Why Did Her Ex Have To Still Be So Attractive?

He made her motor run nonstop whenever he was around. Right now, she couldn't afford to be tempted.

"Don't worry about helping me," she said. She could sense his reluctance. "I changed clothes earlier this evening."

"All right. At least let me put you on the bed before I leave."

Before she could protest, he picked her up as though she were weightless and sat her on the side of the bed.

"I'll see you in the morning," Greg said.

She nodded. He continued to stand there. She closed her eyes. It would be so easy to forget what she'd gone through and accept the here and now....

Dear Reader,

Families have an enormous influence on who we are and how we make our way in the world. I find the dynamics within a family interesting and oftentimes entertaining. Other times I grieve for all the lost opportunities that might have salvaged a relationship.

I hope you enjoy *Married or Not?* and find yourself rooting for each character in his or her struggle for love, happiness and peace.

Sincerely,

Annette Broadrick

ANNETTE BROADRICK

MARRIED OR NOT?

Published by Silhouette Books
America's Publisher of Contemporary Romance

SILHOUETTE BOOKS

ISBN-13: 978-0-373-76840-0
ISBN-10:   0-373-76840-0

MARRIED OR NOT?

Visit Silhouette Books at www.eHarlequin.com

Printed in U.S.A.

ANNETTE BROADRICK

believes in romance and the magic of life. Since 1984, Annette has shared her view of life and love with readers. In addition to being nominated by *Romantic Times BOOKreviews* as one of 1984's Best New Authors, she has also won the following awards from *Romantic Times BOOKreviews:* a Reviewers' Choice Award for Best in its Series; a WISH award; two Lifetime Achievement awards, one for Series Romance and one for Series Romantic Fantasy.

One

If Sherri Masterson had had a crystal ball when she woke up that Friday morning in the middle of May, she would have turned off the alarm and stayed in bed. Instead, she followed her usual routine. She got up and showered at the apartment she shared with Joan Price, who was a schoolteacher. The automatic coffeemaker had her morning beverage waiting for her when she walked into the kitchen. She read the paper, nibbled on a piece of toast and drank her coffee before leaving for work.

Sherri loved her job as a technical writer. She worked in Austin, Texas, with a bunch of brilliant geeks who dreamed up new software for consumers. It was her job to translate computer-speak into plain, everyday language, so that a computer user would have no trouble understanding what the software had to offer and how to use it. She'd worked for New Ideas, Inc., for three years.

When she arrived at the office everyone she met was discussing plans for the weekend.

Her plans were the same every week: do her grocery shopping, take clothes to the dry cleaners and pick up last week's and return home to wash a week's accumulation of clothes, towels and bed linens.

Saturday was the big night of her week when she and her cat would curl up in front of the television and watch a movie rented from Netflix.

She looked forward to her weekends so that she could kick back and enjoy her time off. She wasn't interested in dating, which she had trouble getting across to Joan, who was always trying to fix her up with someone: a fellow teacher, a friend of a friend, even one of the single coaches at her high school.

Sherri wanted none of it: the dating, the possibility of falling in love…again. Getting her heart broken…again. Been there. Done that. Barely survived the aftermath.

However, the point was, she *had* survived. It seemed to be Sherri's lot in life to lose the people she loved and depended upon. She'd discovered that, despite the poet's comment, it was better *not* to love at all than to love and lose.

Sherri had learned that life could be unspeakably cruel three weeks before her fourteenth birthday when she'd been told that the plane carrying her parents home from Greece had crashed.

She'd been staying with her aunt Melanie at the time, and was eager to see her parents again, looking forward to enjoying their photos and, of course, presents and souvenirs they had picked up for her.

She'd talked to her mom every day and lived vicariously through the descriptions of their travels. It had been the first vacation they'd taken on their own. Aunt Melanie had teased them about taking a second honeymoon since they hadn't been able to go anywhere right after their wedding.

When her aunt told her about the crash, Sherri refused to believe that her parents were gone. She'd spoken to them earlier that day. They'd missed her as much as she missed them and finally the separation would be over.

The message must have been wrong. It had to be wrong.

But the crash was covered by all the news networks because the majority of the passengers were Americans and no one survived.

Sherri had little memory of attending the memorial service. Only vignettes of scenes had stayed with her. Her mother's best friend holding her and crying while Sherri stood there, dry eyed. The display of photographs of her parents that her aunt had put together. Her dad's boss telling her aunt that her father had substantial life insurance and a pension plan and that he didn't want Melanie or Sherri to worry about finances.

As though money could begin to replace what she had lost.

She'd been so angry…at everyone: classes that had prevented her from going with her parents, the airline for allowing the plane to crash, and especially her mom and dad for dying and leaving her on her own. She had wished she'd been with them. At least they would all have been together.

Sherri had watched as her home, most of the furniture and furnishings and both cars were sold. She'd told her aunt she didn't want anything from the house, but Melanie knew better and had saved many of the personal belongings that Sherri later came to treasure.

Sherri eventually worked through her grief, but at a price. She learned to keep people at a distance and to refuse offers of help, because depending on others who might leave her was too painful to contemplate. If she didn't let anyone too close, she didn't have to suffer the possibility of enduring another debilitating loss.

She had learned to survive whatever life threw at her without whining and to make tough choices, even if there was a price to pay. Her one attempt, after she'd become an adult, to allow herself to get close to someone had turned out to be a disaster.

Now Sherri concentrated on being an exceptional technical writer and was happy to forgo the painful pleasures of a relationship.

She was engrossed in finishing the technical manual she was working on—the one that had to be at the printer next week—when she heard that her boss, Brad Horton, had called a meeting for ten o'clock that morning.

Nobody seemed to know why. They generally had their meetings on Mondays. She looked at the manuscript with yearning. She was so close to finishing. With any luck the meeting would be short and she could spend the rest of the day finishing and polishing her work.

When she arrived in the conference room, there were fifteen other employees there. Why would Brad call a meeting for a few of them and not the entire work force? Was there some kind of rewards announcement he planned to make?

Sherri looked around the room. There were people from her department as well as from other sections of the company. Maybe all their hard work had paid off. Maybe Brad planned to give them midyear bonuses.

Yeah, right.

None of them had any idea why they were there and the room was buzzing when Brad strode into the room.

"Thank you for being here," he began, his hands clasped behind his back. "As you know, we've been having difficulty meeting our quarterly sales projections. Management has spent considerable time and effort to come up with a solution and we have had to face the reality that the best thing for the company is to lay off some of our employees."

A collective gasp swept the room. Sherri's heart stopped before it began to race. Was he talking about her? She glanced around the table and saw that everyone was looking at him in various degrees of shock.

"I want you to know that none of this has anything to do with your performances," he continued to say as her heart sank. "Each and every one of you is excellent at what you do. It's just that we're being forced to cut costs and unfortunately, this is the only way we can do it."

She was horrified. And embarrassed. No matter how Brad phrased it, each of them was being fired.

Sherri struggled to come to grips with the whole idea. She had never been fired before. Sherri had always received praise for the work she did. Why would they choose to let *her* go? She understood the economics, but why was *she* one of the employees chosen to be laid off?

Her thoughts were bouncing around in her head and she broke out in a cold sweat. What was she going to do? How was she going to face Joan and tell her she'd lost her job? The reason Joan had asked Sherri to be her roommate was because the rent was too much for Joan by herself.

"To make the transition a little easier for each of you…" Brad continued. Sherri forced herself to listen. She had to concentrate. She couldn't display her despair in front of everyone. "…you will each receive a check for two weeks' salary and any vacation leave you have coming.

"You're talented people. Remember that. This is strictly a business decision."

He looked around the room. "Any questions?"

No one spoke. Finally Sherri raised her hand.

"Yes, Sherri?"

"Uh, Brad, you know the manual I've been working on? I've been getting it ready for the printers next week. Do you want me to finish it before I leave?"

He shook his head. "I appreciate your offer, but no. We'll have to deal with this without you." He looked around the room. "Any others?"

No one said anything.

"In that case—" He reached into his coat's breast pocket and pulled out a sheaf of envelopes. "When I call your name please pick up your check from me. There will be someone waiting at your desk to help you clear out your things."

The ultimate humiliation. She would have to clean out her desk while someone looked over her shoulder to make certain she didn't take something that wasn't hers.

With all the dignity she could manage, Sherri walked to the head of the table when her name was called, took her check and returned to her desk. A smile was beyond her.

No one was talking. Those remaining with the company had their heads down, working. Had she been in their place, she would no doubt have done the same. She was now separated from them. They worked here. She didn't.

Numbly she found a box and began to strip her desk of reference books and other odds and ends she'd accumulated over the past three years.

She was escorted out of the building and once in the parking lot, Sherri hurried to her car, at the moment the only escape and sanctuary she had. The inside of the car steamed with heat and she quickly rolled down the windows while she placed the box on the backseat. Inside the car, Sherri placed her hands on the steering wheel and stared blindly through the windshield.

What did I do wrong? I was rarely late and always called in. I didn't take sick days like some of the others. Maybe I shouldn't have skipped that meeting a few weeks ago in order to meet a printing deadline.

Panic surged through her. What about her part of the rent and utilities? She had money put away for emergencies, but nothing like this. She'd have no income to take care of bills.

The money left for her by her parents had enabled Sherri to pay for her college education and to buy herself a car. She'd been thankful not to have to worry about student loans and very grateful for their foresight.

What was she going to do? She had to get another job, but where?

She'd have to go through interviews, which she detested. She'd have to tell them she'd been laid off. Would that be a black mark against her?

Her eyes finally focused on a few people standing near their parked cars, discussing what had happened. She didn't want to discuss what had happened with anyone. What she wanted to do was go back home and hide under the bed, or at least hide her head under her pillow.

Her life had been so carefully structured. She'd believed that working hard and honing her skills would protect her.

Tears trickled down her cheeks. She turned the car on and waited for the air conditioner to blow some cool air before raising the windows.

She couldn't sit in the parking lot all day. She had no place else to go but home. Thank goodness school was still in session. She wouldn't have to face Joan until later today.

Joan planned to spend most of her summer with three of her teacher friends traveling around Europe. They were leaving the latter part of June.

Sherri knew she was being cowardly, but she wished that this could have happened after Joan had left. She could have used the time to pull herself together and make some kind of plans.

She felt sick to her stomach. She had to get through this, somehow.

Sherri flipped the visor down and stared at herself in the mirror. "So. What do you intend to do now?"

The image in the mirror, with its dark-brown hair, green eyes and pasty white skin stared back blankly.

"Try not to panic. You can do this."

She flipped the mirror up and eased the car forward. As she pulled out of the parking lot, Sherri thought of one positive…at least her car was paid for. That was one less worry. It was a few years old but she took good care of it. She only prayed nothing major broke down until she had a steady income once again.

She glanced back for a moment before getting on the access road of the freeway. Happiness was *not* looking in your rearview mirror to see the building where you no longer worked.

Sherri followed the access road until she could merge with traffic on the highway. She glanced at the car clock, amazed to discover it wasn't even noon yet. Had it only been a few hours ago that she'd been home sipping coffee and reading the paper?

She shook her head. There was definitely a time warp going on. Nothing seemed real to her.

Once on the highway, Sherri headed for home. Traffic flowed smoothly at this time of day, which was a blessing. She had to force herself to focus on her driving.

After a few miles of traveling at seventy, she realized that, once again, luck was against her. Brake lights showed up ahead of her and she began to slow down. There must be an accident up ahead.

Out of habit, she glanced in her rearview mirror and froze.

A tractor-trailer rig had suddenly appeared at the top of the rise behind her and was bearing down on her.

Couldn't he see all the red brake lights ahead of him? Couldn't he see that she had come to a complete stop?

Time slowed down for her as she watched him attempt to slow down his rig. She could hear his brakes screaming as he moved inexorably toward her.

Sherri felt a certain calm fall upon her as she waited for him to hit her. Maybe this was the way her life would end. At that moment, she really didn't care.

The last thing she remembered was the sound of screeching metal as the rig plowed into her car.

Sherri roused at some point, wondering where she was. She felt as though she were floating. She vaguely heard voices that didn't seem to have anything to do with her. Excited voices. She lazily wondered what they were excited about.

A voice near her head yelled. "This one's trapped in her car. We've gotta get her out of here. Now!"

"Is she alive?"

"Can't tell. I can see her, but can't reach her.

She wondered who they were talking about.

Loud sounds echoed around her, which was irritating. How rude. Couldn't they see she was trying to rest?

She faded away, the voices in the distance, until she felt a hand at her throat.

"There's a pulse. Let's get her out of there."

The seat shifted. Why was she under the dash? Compact cars were too small to be playing games.

Then more hands touched her, moving her.

She screamed and blacked out once again.

Two

Greg Hogan was returning to the police station when dispatch called him to come in. As a homicide detective, he spent as little time at the station as possible. As it happened, though, today he needed to run some information through the station's computer. He was investigating the murder of a young photographer, and evidence he had gathered pointed to a person who knew his victim well enough to have invited him into his home. He had a couple of suspects in mind. Now he had to follow up on some leads in order to get the necessary evidence for an arrest.

He wondered why he'd been called in. Maybe he'd irritated the captain. If so, it would only be the third time this week. The captain didn't like Greg's attitude toward work. He wasn't a team player. He was a maverick. The problem was, Greg solved homicides and the captain had trouble arguing with his success.

Not that Greg's success ever stopped the captain from

griping at him. Greg had grown so used to it that he'd long ago tuned him out, figuring that while the captain was going after Greg, he was leaving the others under his command alone.

Last week Pete Carter had pointed out how altruistic Greg was, protecting the other men from the captain. Pete was a sergeant on the force and had been around longer than any of them. Greg promptly suggested that since all the men were better off with him taking the brunt of the tongue-lashings, they owed him a beer. And darned if they hadn't taken him out one night and wouldn't let him pay for anything.

Greg smiled at the memory.

He pulled into his parking space at the station and got out of his car. The parking space was one of the perks he'd received with his promotion to lieutenant a few months ago, despite the prickly relationship he had with the captain.

Life was good.

As soon as Greg walked inside, he knew something was wrong. There were more men standing around in the bull pen than usual. And all of them looked grim. Greg put his hands on his hips.

"What's going on?"

Pete walked over to him and put his hand on his shoulder. "Greg, I'm afraid I have some bad news for you."

Greg looked around the room and frowned. "What happened? Did one of the guys get hurt? Who?"

"No. It's Sherri."

"Sherri? What about her?"

"She was in a multicar accident this morning. They airlifted her to the hospital…alive when they got her to the hospital, but I heard she was in critical condition."

Greg was thankful there was a chair nearby. His knees

shook so hard he sank into the chair before his reaction became apparent to everyone. He clenched his jaw.

"I figured that since the two of you had some history together that you'd want to know," Pete went on, sounding sympathetic.

Greg shook his head, feeling dazed. He pushed his hand through his hair and forced himself to look at Pete. "They're sure it was her?"

"Yeah. A semi jackknifed when he tried to stop on the freeway and he plowed into her. She was in the last car of a string of them that were stopped due to an earlier accident. Six vehicles were in the smash-up and there were serious injuries in several of the cars, but she caught the brunt of it."

Greg closed his eyes. Sherri? Near death? Couldn't be.

"What hospital?" he finally asked.

Pete told him.

"Thanks for letting me know," Greg said, and left.

He drove to the hospital on autopilot. He parked near the emergency entrance and strode across the parking lot. Inside, the place teemed with people; doctors and nurses moved among patients with various injuries. It looked like a war zone, with some of the injured on stretchers and others in chairs. The Emergency Medical Technicians from the various ambulances outside were working on those victims not as severely injured as the ones they'd brought in.

He quickly checked each stretcher and when he didn't see her, went over to the nurses' station.

"I'm looking for one of the accident victims who were air-lifted to this hospital. Sherri Masterson Hogan."

The harried nurse said, "Sir, you can see that we're over-whelmed with all the injuries here and—"

"Just tell me where they took her and I'll be out of here."

She hurried past him, shaking her head.

He turned around and faced the noise and confusion around him. He knew he wouldn't get any answers here.

Greg continued down the hallway, ignoring signs that read Do Not Enter and shoving doors open, looking into each cubicle for signs of her. A member of the hospital staff stopped him. Greg checked his name tag, which read Dr. Luke Davis, and figured he was one of the doctors on duty.

"Sir, I must ask you to return to the waiting area. Someone will help you as soon as possible."

Greg said as clearly as he could with his jaws clenched, "Dr. Davis. I'm looking for Sherri Masterson Hogan, who was in that six-car smash-up. I'm told she was airlifted here and I intend to find her."

The doctor nodded. "I see. Are you a family member?"

"I'm her husband."

What difference did it make, anyway? He was determined to see her, regardless of their relationship.

"Hold on. I'll see what I can find out for you," Dr. Davis said, striding down the hallway, the tails of his medical coat flapping around him.

Greg paced back and forth, dodging carts, beds and medical personnel until the doctor returned.

"She's in surgery."

"What are her injuries?"

Dr. Davis shook his head. "You'll need to speak to the surgeon about that."

"Where can I find him when he gets out of surgery?"

"You can wait for him upstairs, in Intensive Care. He'll look for family members when he finishes."

Greg swallowed. "I want to see her as soon as possible."

"The surgeon will discuss that with you."

Greg nodded, turned on his heel and headed toward the bank of elevators.

"Good luck," Dr. Davis said behind him.

Greg rode the elevator to the next floor where the ICU was located. It was quiet on the ICU floor, which was a relief from the pandemonium downstairs. He pushed through double swinging doors and found the nurses' station.

"Sir," one of the nurses said, "you can't come in here."

"I'm waiting for Sherri Masterson Hogan to come out of surgery."

She looked down at the desk and riffled through some files. She read some of the files before saying, "We have a Sherri Masterson who has been recently admitted."

So she'd taken back her maiden name. Why wasn't he surprised?

"Are you family?"

He'd already lied once. "Her husband."

She nodded. "Good. We need to get more information on her."

He took a deep breath. "Okay."

She went down a list, asking questions. He knew her age, birthdate, even her blood type, but he had no idea where she lived these days, so he rattled off his own address.

After answering the rest of the questions, Greg wandered down the hallway to the ICU waiting room with the nurse's promise that the doctor would be out to speak with him as soon as he was out of surgery.

Greg hated sitting around, but he had no intention of leaving the hospital until he knew more about Sherri's injuries.

He wondered why he cared. He hadn't seen or spoken to her in almost two years. Eighteen months, six days, to be precise.

She'd asked him not to contact her once everything had ended, and he'd determinedly followed her instructions. He'd almost convinced himself she was part of his past. He was so over her. Then what was he doing here? Why had he panicked at the thought that she could die?

For one thing, she was much too young, six years younger than his thirty-two years.

Just because she wanted no part of me didn't mean she deserved to die.

The last six months they were together had been filled with so much tension that it had become a third party in their marriage. She'd withdrawn into herself. When he asked what was wrong, she told him that he was too secretive about his past and his background. She said she didn't really know him at all.

Okay, so he wasn't the most talkative person in the world…especially about his feelings. He'd never been good about opening himself up and sharing his innermost thoughts and emotions with anyone.

When they'd first married, she had asked him all kinds of questions…about his childhood, his family, why he'd chosen to be a cop. He never liked talking about his childhood or his family and admittedly he was less than forthcoming. As far as he was concerned, all of that was in the past and had no bearing on who he was today. He'd just had trouble explaining that to Sherri's satisfaction. He'd finally stopped trying.

He shouldn't have been all that surprised the day he got home to find every last trace of her presence in his apartment gone. She'd left the key to his place on the counter with a note telling him that she was getting a divorce and to contact her attorney—she also left the attorney's business card—if he had any questions.

Hell yes, he'd had questions! How could she just move out like that? She'd kept asking him to talk to her about stupid things, but that was no reason just to walk out on him. He'd loved her and she'd thrown his love back in his face. Why else would she have hired an attorney before she'd even bothered to tell him she wanted a divorce?

He'd been furious with her. He'd waited three days to calm down enough to call her attorney, who had told him that since they'd acquired no property of significance during the three years of their marriage, Sherri wanted to keep what was hers and let him keep what was his.

He hadn't argued because he knew there would be no point. She'd obviously made up her mind and his opinion didn't matter.

He'd tried to be what she'd wanted in a husband, but he hadn't really known what she expected a husband to be. He'd been alone for most of his twenty-seven years before they'd met. Of course there had been adjustments to sharing a place with her. However, he'd loved her and showed his love in every way he knew how, but his love hadn't been enough. He knew, was absolutely convinced, that she'd loved him in the beginning. There was no way she could have faked her response to him. His off-duty hours had been spent in bed with her, making love to her, holding her, listening to her while she talked about her childhood and her family.

She'd had it tough and he'd told her that he would always be there for her, that he would never abandon her, or leave her to deal with life on her own.

And yet…

After a while she'd stopped talking to him as much and he figured that was because she'd told him everything about her past. She would ask him about his work, but once he was home he didn't want to talk about his job. He just wanted to be with her.

He'd always worked long hours during an investigation, but she'd known that. He might have rushed her into marriage a little fast, but he had been afraid he would lose her if he settled for a long engagement. He'd lost her anyway.

Well, he'd come to terms with the divorce. There wasn't much else he could do. He'd tried to console himself that cops had a higher rate of failed relationships than almost any other profession. Somehow, that hadn't helped him get over the pain of losing her.

And now she was seriously injured. Regardless of the circumstances, he could not leave the hospital without knowing how she was.

Greg waited three more hours before a weary doctor wearing scrubs appeared in the doorway. "Mr. Masterson?"

"Um, no. Greg Hogan. Sherri uses her maiden name." He had trouble talking around the knot in his throat. He finally managed to ask, "How is she?"

The doctor rubbed the back of his neck. "There was some internal bleeding and we had to remove her spleen. She's in stable condition. I think she's going to get through this with no problem. The airbag saved her life but there was some bruising. Her right arm is broken as well as her right leg, so she'll be slowed down for a while, but otherwise, I think she's in good shape, considering what she went through."

Greg's relief at the news caused him to choke up. He rubbed the bridge of his nose with his thumb and forefinger, trying to gain control over his emotions.

"May I see her?" he finally managed to ask.

"She's in recovery at the moment. Once they move her to ICU one of the nurses will come get you."

"Thank you." Greg held out his hand and the surgeon shook it before leaving the room.

Broken bones. Those would heal. The trauma caused by the surgery would also need time to heal. She was going to be okay. He fought the constriction in his throat. He was tired, that's all.

He glanced at his watch. It was after six and he still hadn't followed up on the investigation he was conducting. The team needed answers quickly. Law-enforcement personnel knew that the first forty-eight hours after a crime was committed were the most critical for gathering evidence. He needed to get back on this one before any more time was lost.

He approached the nurse who had taken down the information on Sherri. "May I help you?" she asked.

"Do you have any idea when Sherri Masterson will be out of recovery?"

"Not really." She shook her head. "They'll keep her in recovery until her vitals stabilize."

When would that be? Soon, he hoped. He really needed to see her.

"I have to get back to work right now, but I'll definitely be back later tonight."

The nurse nodded and Greg headed for the elevators. He'd started to shake once the doctor had left. Reaction and relief that her injuries were no longer life-threatening and that she'd made it through surgery all right had gotten to him.

There was nothing he could do for her at this point, a feeling he'd often had when they were together. That didn't mean that he could just walk away from her now.

Three

Greg returned to the hospital a little after midnight. Another shift was at the nurses' station.

He'd managed to get some work done on his latest investigation before he'd gone to find Sherri's car. What he'd seen had sickened him and caused him to wonder how she had survived.

"I'm Sherri Masterson's husband, Greg Hogan," he said quietly. "I haven't been able to see her since her surgery. Would it be possible to see her now?"

An older nurse came around the counter. "Follow me. Please don't stay long."

"Has she been awake at all since coming to the ICU?"

"For a few minutes when they brought her to her room. She's being given something for pain and is pretty groggy."

Greg hadn't known what to expect when he walked into her room. He hadn't seen her in almost two years, but nothing could have prepared him for the shock of seeing her lying there so still.

He wouldn't have recognized her. Her face was swollen, with cuts and bruises that no doubt occurred when her airbag inflated.

The hospital staff had her hooked up to machines and a bag of liquid. One machine monitored her heart, another kept track of her blood pressure and pulse and he knew the drip contained saline solution to keep her hydrated.

She was so pale that if it hadn't been for the steady beat of the machine, he would have thought she was dead.

He'd forgotten how small she was because she had loomed so large in his memory.

Her thick lashes lay on her cheeks hiding her amazingly green eyes. She looked peaceful lying with her arms beside her. Her dark hair framed her face and he realized she'd cut it. Now it feathered around her head. Her poor face was battered and she had a black eye but all of that would go away with time and rest.

He stepped closer to the bed and placed her limp hand in his.

"What have you done to yourself, Sherri?" he whispered. "What were you doing out on the highway in the middle of the day? Had you gotten sick at work and gone home early?"

She stirred and her lashes fluttered, but her eyes stayed closed.

The nurse returned to the room. "You'll need to leave now. I'm sure she'll be more awake in the morning."

The next morning Greg was at the hospital by seven o'clock. He found Sherri sleeping. One of the nurses came in.

"How's she doing?" he asked, his voice low.

"Remarkably well, considering. She roused a few times in the night while we were checking on her but went back to sleep. Rest is the best thing for her. "

Sherri heard people talking nearby. She wished they would go away and let her sleep. The alarm hadn't gone off yet to remind her to get up. They continued to talk and Sherri could have sworn she recognized one of the voices: a deep voice that had always made her heart race.

"Greg?" she whispered. Surely not. Why would he—

"I'm right here, Sherri," he replied, picking up her hand and bringing it to his lips.

She was probably dreaming, but why would she dream of him?

Finally, she opened her eyes and stared at him. "Greg?" she whispered in wonder. "Is it you?" She remembered now that she was in the hospital. What was he doing there?

He nodded and flashed a brief smile at her. "How are you feeling?" He sat in the chair next to her bed.

She looked at her hand still nestled in his. "Very strange. I think I'm actually dreaming this conversation."

"No, I'm really here. I've been worried about you."

"I must be in worse shape than I thought if you're here," she said roughly, her mouth dry.

Without hesitation he reached over and handed her a bottle of water with a plastic straw in it.

She sipped on the water, trying to bring her brain into some kind of focus.

He brushed her hair off her forehead. "You cut your hair."

"Yes. It's easier to keep this way."

Neither one of them spoke after that. Sherri couldn't come up with a coherent thought or question.

"Do you remember the accident?" he finally asked.

"No. I guess I got a little banged up."

"Some internal injuries and a broken arm and leg would bear that out."

"The doctor said he had to remove my spleen and sew up some tears inside." She paused before saying, "No more gymnastics for me, I guess." He didn't smile, which didn't surprise her. It was a lame joke.

"My guess is that the seat belt did its job and saved your life but caused damage of its own."

She had trouble keeping her eyes off him. Greg Hogan was there in the hospital to see her. They'd had no contact in years and yet, now he was here.

"This is too weird. Why are you here?"

"I told you."

"How did you hear about the accident?"

"At the station. That was one heck of a pile-up and several units were out there. Someone radioed in that your car had been sandwiched between an eighteen-wheeler and an SUV." He nodded toward the nearby table. "They brought your purse back to the station when they recognized you and gave it to me. I left it here when I checked on you last night."

She closed her eyes for a moment. "Sorry," she said. "I'm having trouble concentrating on anything. I feel like I'm floating."

"It's the meds they're giving you. You're going to be fine, you know."

"That's good," she murmured.

Greg watched her go back to sleep and smiled. He'd turned over his cases to some of the other detectives and asked for time off. He wanted to be here in case she needed him. She had no family since her aunt had died and he didn't want her to be alone.

Of course he knew he had no business being there. She'd made it more than clear when she left him that she no longer wanted him around her. He picked up on the fact that she was less than thrilled to see him there, honestly puzzled, and he couldn't explain to her what he couldn't explain to himself.

He just knew that he had to be there. He leaned back in the chair and closed his eyes. He hadn't gotten much sleep last night. Now he waited until she woke up again.

The next time Sherri opened her eyes and saw him, she frowned. "You're still here."

He nodded.

"I don't understand. Aren't you supposed to be at work?"

"I took some time off."

"You said you talked to some of the men who were at the scene of the accident. Did they say how badly my car was damaged?"

"There's not much left of it, I'm afraid. It's a miracle you survived. When I saw it, I didn't know how you could have come out of it alive."

"It can't be repaired?" she asked wistfully.

"'Fraid not." He rubbed her knuckles with his thumb. "I'm sorry. I know how much you loved that little car."

Tears welled into her eyes. "I'm being silly to cry over a stupid car. It's just that it was my very first car and I bought it brand-new."

"I spoke to your roommate a little while ago while you were asleep. She didn't know you'd been in an accident until late last night. When she called the hospital this morning to find out how you were, the nurse forwarded the call to your room. I guess the hospital will only give out information to family members."

"You're not family." Tears continued to slide down her cheeks.

"But the hospital doesn't know that. I told them I was your husband."

She started to sit up and then grabbed her tummy and winced.

"Easy. You've just had major surgery."

"Why would you lie like that?"

"Like I said," he began patiently. "The hospital won't give

out information on a patient except to family members. I needed to know how you were doing so I told them we were married. I had this same conversation with Joan. She'd never heard of me." He cocked his head and looked at her, his brows raised.

"I never told her your name. All she knows is that I'm divorced."

"I think she was surprised to find me here."

Sherri almost smiled. "I'm sure she was." More tears flowed. "I didn't get a chance to tell her."

"Tell her what?"

"About what happened. I lost my job yesterday."

"So that's why you were on the highway at that time of day."

She sighed. "It was definitely a Black Friday for me."

She kept wiping away her tears. He took a tissue and wiped her cheeks.

"The important thing is that you're alive. You can always get another car and another job."

She glanced down at her body. "Right. With my arm and leg in casts, I have a hunch a prospective employer would not be impressed."

"You don't need to find a job next week, you know. You're going to need time to rest and recuperate."

She shook her head. "You don't understand. I'm obligated to pay half the bills for our apartment. Joan depends on me just as I depend on her."

"Joan wondered how you'd be able to climb the stairs to your apartment, which I think is a fair question. You can't handle crutches until your arm heals and that would be at least six weeks."

"Oh, no! I hadn't gotten around to thinking about that." She shook her head. "I can't believe all of this happened in one day."

"Did you get a severance check?"

She nodded toward her purse. "I hope it's still in there."

"May I look?" he asked, reaching for it.

She closed her eyes. "I suppose. I don't seem to have any secrets from you."

He saw the crumpled envelope just inside the purse. He handed it to her. "Is this it?"

She opened her eyes and looked first at the envelope and then at him. "With one arm in a sling and the other hooked up to a drip, I can't even take it."

"I'll put it in the bank for you if you like. I'll need a deposit slip."

"Also in my purse."

He found her checkbook and without looking at the balance, tore off a deposit slip and put it back in her purse.

When he looked back at her she was staring at him. She didn't say anything, just looked at him. After a lengthy silence, he finally asked, "What?"

"I still don't understand why you're here."

"I care about you."

She sounded frustrated when she replied, "I don't understand why."

He smiled. "I've gotta admit, it surprised me, too."

Her eyes drooped.

"Get some sleep. I'll come back later."

"You don't have to. I'm okay."

"Yes, I know. Just humor me, okay?"

Her eyes closed and he waited for her to say something, but she didn't. She'd fallen asleep.

He stroked her hand as he studied her. He was glad to see she had a little more color in her face.

Greg stroked her cheek and whispered, "Take care of yourself, little one," and walked out of the room.

Four

Two days later Sherri woke up in a panic. She'd been having a nightmare, or perhaps her subconscious had chosen to relive some of her worst moments. She looked around her room and saw that she was alone.

She realized she was holding her breath and let it out with a whoosh, her relief overwhelming. The nightmare had probably been the result of knowing that she was being released from the hospital today. Somehow she would have to navigate the stairs to her second-story apartment. Once there, she would be something of a captive until her leg cast came off.

At the moment, getting to her apartment wasn't her worst problem. How could she look for work like this? No one in his or her right mind would hire her. She wasn't even sure she could work full-time right away. She'd been in good shape, relatively speaking, but she was a long way from getting over the wreck. Her little car was gone. Her insurance would only pay a percentage of her hospital bills, which were going to be astronomical. For that matter, she might not have any insurance. Had it been canceled the day she was laid off? She hoped it had been in effect until midnight of that day. She'd paid her part of the insurance premiums for the entire month and, as if all of that wasn't enough to deal with, she also had Greg to contend with.

He'd come by to see her for both of the past two days. She didn't want him here. She'd hoped never to see him again. Why? Because she still turned to mush whenever she was around him. That was the reason she had asked him to leave her alone after the divorce. She could deal with the hurt and the pain of the divorce as long as it was a distant memory. As soon as she saw him she was instantly reminded of how much in love she'd been with him, and how much he'd hurt her.

One of the things she found attractive about him when they'd first met was that he was a man of action and didn't talk much. Clams were chattier, she was sure. She hadn't understood then that without open communication between them, their marriage could not succeed.

Granted, she didn't expect him to talk about his work. She understood that. Eventually, they didn't talk at all. She couldn't live that way. He knew her entire life history. She knew little about his background or past. She understood that there were people who hated to talk about themselves, but Greg had carried his reticence to an extreme.

What had ended the marriage as far as she was concerned was that she'd discovered he'd lied to her. Flat-out lied. The other things had been tough enough to deal with, but when she'd found out the truth about him and that he had hidden it from her for their entire marriage, she knew she could no longer live with him.

And yet… He'd heard about her accident and had come to see her. Okay. She could understand that a little. I mean, they had known each other intimately at one time. She supposed he could have been concerned about her.

However, she was at a loss to figure out why he came each day to see her. It was ridiculous. They had little to talk about. She certainly had no intention of getting involved in his life again.

Each time he'd left she'd politely told him not to come back. He came anyway.

Well, if he showed up today she'd give up the polite part and tell him to leave her alone. If he didn't show up, she'd be gone. As far as she knew, he didn't know where she lived— No. Wait. He'd said something about her living on the second floor. He couldn't know that if he hadn't been by there.

Well, when she saw him, she intended to set him straight. She did not want him in her life in any way. Thanks for the offer, but no thanks. She hoped that the meeting would happen later rather than sooner. She needed to get her strength back before facing him. Otherwise, she might end up throwing herself into his arms crying, "Save me! Save me!"

Not her style at all, but then whenever she was around Greg, she had trouble thinking coherently.

The aide came in with her breakfast. "The doctor wants to check to see how you are this morning. He's making rounds now, so it shouldn't be too long." She set the tray on the rolling table. "Enjoy."

Sherri looked at the tray. Enjoy. Right. Clear liquids. No coffee. She had to be on a special diet until everything damaged inside her healed. She'd have to give Joan a list of the things she could eat and have her bring them home. It would be good to get home and let Lucifer, her cat, love her.

Or rather push his head into her hand to love him. He was company, all the company she needed.

She began to eat, resigned to the diet for now.

Greg pulled into the parking lot of the hospital. Sherri was being dismissed today and he already knew she wasn't going to like what he'd done.

Too bad. Like it or not, she would have to accept that this was the way things would be for the foreseeable future.

Greg saw her doctor as soon as he stepped off the elevator. Dr. Hudson stood at the nurses' station, going over a chart with one of the nurses.

Greg waited until the two were finished and walked over. "Good morning, Dr. Hudson. I understand Sherri is being moved today," he said as he approached the doctor.

"Yes. I was just in there. She's doing well, considering, but will still need plenty of rest. The bones should knit back together with no problem. My only concern would be that she might start hemorrhaging. I wouldn't leave her alone for the next several days."

"No problem."

Greg nodded, his mind racing. He walked to the open door of Sherri's room and knocked on the jamb. When she glanced up, he walked inside, his hands in his pockets.

She scowled. "What are you doing here? I thought I made it clear that you don't need to keep checking on me. I'm fine."

"Ah. You must be feeling better."

"I am. In fact, I'm going home today."

"Good for you."

"So you don't need to worry about me."

"Okay."

"I'm waiting for the nurse to come help me dress. So if you'll excuse me…"

"Want me to help? I'm right here and it wouldn't be the first time I've helped you to dress…or undress."

Her sigh was filled with frustration. "No, Greg. I do not need your help to dress or undress. Thank you for coming but—"

"But don't let the door hit me in the—"

"Goodbye, Greg."

He shrugged and walked out of the room. Hoo-boy. His powers of persuasion better kick in really fast or he was going to be in bigger trouble than he already was.

He'd finally had to face his real motive in helping her. The fact that she had no family was part of the reason, but the hard fact was that he was in still in love with her. He was supposed to be completely over her by now. Instead, he hadn't wanted to leave her side since the accident. Once he realized that his feelings for her had never changed, he knew that he would provide whatever she needed to heal, whether or not she was comfortable with his help.

After signing her release papers, Sherri was placed in a wheelchair and taken to the lobby. When she looked outside, she didn't see her cab. Well, it should be here soon.

"You can leave me here by the door while I wait for my taxi," she said to the nurse.

The woman looked at her as though she'd lost her mind. "I don't think so," the nurse replied. As the automatic doors opened for them, the nurse continued, "You aren't going home in a taxi, honey. Your husband is taking you home."

The doors closed behind them as Sherri whipped her head around. She saw Greg, leaning against a black sports car parked at the front entrance, his arms folded over his chest, his ankles crossed. At the moment he was in profile, gazing across the parking lot.

Panic set in. "He's not my husband!"

The nurse chuckled. "Well, that's good to know. Then can I have him? Whoever he is, he's here to take you home, according to your discharge papers." She continued to push Sherri's chair toward Greg.

Greg saw them and straightened. He wore wrap-around sunglasses and still had on the dazzling white T-shirt and snug-fitting jeans he'd worn earlier. He'd finished off his haute couture ensemble with sneakers that might have been white in a far-distant past.

"What are you doing here?" she said.

"I am here to whisk you away in my chariot, milady," he said with a bow.

"That really isn't necessary," she said, looking over her shoulder at the nurse, intending to ask the woman to take her back to the lobby. The only problem was that the nurse was staring at Greg with a dazed grin on her face.

Sherri quickly ran through her options and realized that she had been outmaneuvered. She rubbed her forehead where an ache began to throb. "Great," she muttered, and said nothing more while Greg and the man-hungry nurse helped her into his car.

Once inside, she stared straight ahead pretending he wasn't there, which was a little difficult to do when he leaned over and carefully fastened her seat belt. "I know you're glad to be out of the hospital. No one can sleep well with all the activity going on."

She didn't reply. There was no way she could interact with him and keep her distance, and it was essential that she remain distant.

They'd been driving for about ten minutes when she broke her silence. "Wait!"

"For what?"

"This isn't the way to my apartment."

"I know."

"What are you doing, kidnapping me?"

"Nothing so dramatic. I thought you might like to go to Barton Springs and enjoy the sunshine."

"Greg, it's a hundred degrees today."

"We'll park in the shade."

The pounding in her head intensified.

He found shade and pulled beneath one of the huge live oak trees. He left the engine and air conditioning running while he removed his seat belt and turned to her.

"I know I'm the very last person you want in your life, now or at any other time. I get that. I just want to give you a chance to look over your options."

She sighed. "They're extremely limited."

"Not necessarily." He paused, cleared his throat and finally continued. "Please hear me out before you say anything. Okay?"

She just looked at him.

"I spoke to Joan a couple of days ago about your situation. We agreed that you can't stay at the apartment. With no elevator you would be trapped up there. It isn't safe and it could be quite dangerous."

She lowered her head, not wanting to look at him. "Then why didn't Joan tell me herself? I've talked to her every day."

"I asked her to let me talk to you about everything."

"You mean there's more?" she asked, wishing her voice didn't sound as though she were on the edge of hysteria.

"Yeah. There is. Joan will be leaving in a few weeks—"

"I know that! She's been planning this trip for two years!"

"Yes, well, then you probably don't want her to cancel the trip," he replied smoothly.

"Of course I don't. I don't need her to look after me."

"That isn't the point. Without your paying half the bills on the apartment, she'll need the money she set aside for her holiday to pay all of them."

Sherri slumped in her seat and closed her eyes.

"My suggestion was that she get another roommate, which she has done."

Her eyes flew open. "You did what? Are you out of your mind? I no longer have a job. I no longer have a car. And, thanks to you, I don't even have a place to live? Gee, thanks, Greg. You've certainly made my day. Maybe you'd better drop me off at the Salvation Army. I understand they look after the homeless with no jobs."

She hadn't realized how loud she'd gotten until she stopped. Her voice still rang around them. She took several deep breaths. *I can get through this. Somehow, some way, I can do this. I've got friends. I've got...what, exactly? A broken arm and leg and I'm presently recovering from surgery. Oh, yeah. I'm in really great shape.*

After a silence that stretched between them for several minutes, he asked, "Are you through?"

Oh, how she'd love to brain him over the head with her cast. With her luck, she'd probably break her arm again.

"Yes," she muttered, looking out the side window so he wouldn't see the tears that filled her eyes.

"What I think would work out best for you is to stay with me until, quite literally, you get back on your feet."

She whipped her head around to stare at him so fast she'd probably added whiplash to her other injuries.

Horrified by the suggestion, she could only stare at him.

So many thoughts raced through her mind that her head was spinning. The whole world had gone mad. Or at least her tiny part of it. Didn't he know it would be impossible for her to live with him again? Was he so insensitive to her feelings that he didn't understand how painful being around him would be for her?

She settled on one major objection that she'd already heard him explain about her apartment. "You live in a second-story apartment, too."

"I've moved."

"When? Yesterday?"

She saw his lips twitch. She was glad somebody was enjoying this nightmare.

"About three months ago."

"Good for you." She gazed out over the park. She could hear splashing from a nearby pool and saw people sitting in the shade. What she wanted to do was to get out of the car and walk away. And she couldn't.

She was well and truly trapped by her own circumstances.

"Not really."

"The move didn't work out the way you hoped?"

"My great-grandmother died a few months ago and left me her home."

"Oh, no! Millie's dead?"

"Well, she was in her nineties, after all. She didn't suffer. She just didn't wake up one morning."

"Oh, Greg. I am so sorry. You were so close to her."

"Yeah, I know." He waited a couple of beats and said, "Here's what I would like to do, if you'll allow it. As you know, there's plenty of room for you and me to stay in the same house and never see each other. Once your casts are gone you can get back some of your muscle strength using the pool.

"Your doctor said that it would be a while before you'd be able to get along on your own. It makes more sense for you to stay at my place until you're mobile. You'll be comfortable there and I'll be available if you need help."

She knew she would need help. She still had trouble dressing, and getting a shower would be a major ordeal. But there was no way she would accept that kind of help from Greg.

Sherri shook her head. "It's kind of you to offer, Greg, and quite generous considering the history between us. Sharing a place, no matter the size, would be tantamount to living together again and I can't do that." She looked away and repeated softly, "I really can't do that."

"Then where do you want me to take you?"

She rubbed her forehead where her headache had intensified. "I don't have any idea, but I need to lie down somewhere. I can stay at your place until I figure out what I'm going to do, I suppose." She'd be living a nightmare until she was able to find a place to rent. She had enough savings to pay for all the deposits and the first and last month's rent if she was very careful. After that, she'd be without resources.

"Of course," he said, pulling out of the parking space. "I know you've been through a terrible ordeal and this is far from being a perfect option, but it was the only one I could come up with for now."

"Having you come back into my life when I'm in this condition hasn't helped, believe me," she said, rubbing her forehead.

She saw his jaw clench, but she was too exhausted to care if she'd been too blunt. Her emotions had been all over the place since she had seen him standing beside his car today and had discovered that he wasn't going to be out of her life. At the time, she'd thought she could hold out another few hours. Not days or possibly weeks.

"Nice wheels. Did they come with the house?"

"The house came with a tidy sum from a trust fund."

"It must be nice having money," she muttered bitterly.

"Not necessarily," he said in response.

They rode the rest of the way in silence. She recognized the neighborhood and thought about the times they'd visited Millie when they were married. She'd thought Millie was the only family Greg had. In fact, he'd told her Millie *was* his only family and she had been able to relate to being raised without parents.

Once Sherri had left Greg, she'd missed seeing the elderly lady. It would be strange to be in her house when she wasn't there.

"Is Lorraine still there?"

"No. After Millie died, she said she wanted to retire. She'd looked after Millie for many years and Millie left her enough to live on in comfort."

They pulled into a long driveway that ended at a three-car garage behind the large home.

Greg walked around and opened her door. She hadn't thought about how she would get into the house because, frankly, too many other things were going on in her head.

He reached inside the car and effortlessly picked her up. There was nothing for her to do except put her arms around his neck. She was at the end of her stamina. All she could do was lie against his chest and close her eyes.

Millie's place was so beautiful with its colorful flower beds and shrubs. Once inside the gate between the high privacy hedges, the view opened up to reveal a pristine lawn spotted with large trees and an Olympic-size pool.

"Millie always enjoyed her pool," she murmured to herself. She closed her eyes again.

"She kept herself in great shape. Probably why she lived as long as she did."

A wide expanse of floor-length windows and French doors looked out over the vista. As Greg stepped up onto the redbrick terrace, a woman opened one of the doors.

"Ah, Hannah," Greg said, smiling. "Thank you for opening the door." He looked at Sherri. "This is Sherri. Sherri, Hannah."

So he was married. He could have mentioned that when she was going on and on about their living together. He must have found her quite amusing.

He could have told her at some point. It made no difference to their relationship, or rather lack of relationship. Sherri was glad to know that he'd found someone else. She didn't know why she was so surprised. He was handsome, well-educated and now could give any woman whatever she wanted.

Being this close to him was so disturbing. He wore the same aftershave, the one that had haunted her for months after she'd left.

Greg carried her through the wide hallway toward the front of the house. A wide, curving staircase went up to the second floor. Before they reached the stairs, Greg stopped in front of a closed door.

He gathered her closer, if possible, and opened the door. This had been Millie's room. She remembered it well. Millie's light perfume still lingered. A motorized wheelchair was near the bed. She wondered if Millie had needed it during her last few months. If so, Sherri knew Millie would have hated to be confined to a chair.

He carefully placed her on the bed and stepped back. "I'll be right back."

She closed her eyes and was drifting in a sea of pain when she felt something move on the bed. Her eyes popped open and she gasped. Two cats had jumped on the bed and were daintily stepping up to her.

"Where did you two come from?" she asked them in astonishment.

Greg said from the doorway, "When Joan mentioned that you had planned to take care of both cats while she was gone, I volunteered to keep them here, since she didn't want to split them up."

He handed her a glass of water and two capsules. She recognized the pain meds from the hospital.

"How did you know I was taking these?"

He shrugged. "I got a list of your medications from the doctor."

Sherri swallowed the capsules, chased them with the water and lay down again. She was grateful that these were fast acting.

After a moment of silence, Greg said, "I forgot to ask Joan their names."

"This is Lucifer," she replied. Lucifer reached her side and butted his head against her hand, purring all the while.

"So is this one Satan?" he asked with a teasing glint in his eye, a look she'd always loved.

"No. Angel." She glanced at Angel. He had lifted his back leg and was now engrossed in cleaning himself.

She scratched Lucifer's ears and under his chin until he settled in next to her, his front legs across her chest. Sherri looked up at Greg. "You hate cats."

He stood watching her from the foot of the four-poster bed, his hands in his back pockets. "Yep." He smiled. "Looks like he's missed you."

"Why would you accept the care and feeding of animals you don't like?"

He stood there and looked at her, as though he could see her soul and understood all her emotions. Which was impossible.

"Good question," he finally replied thoughtfully. "So far, I haven't found a sensible answer." He turned away and headed for the door. "Get some rest," he said over his shoulder, leaving the room and closing the door behind him.

When Sherri opened her eyes sometime later the room was in deep shadow. She noticed that the sun was beyond the treetops. She must have slept all day. She looked around her and saw the two cats still on the bed and sound asleep.

Lucifer enjoyed stretching out on his back as far as his long legs would go. Angel preferred sleeping in a ball. One was on either side of her.

A small lamp came on near the door and Sherri saw Hannah standing in the doorway.

"I'm sorry to disturb you, but you didn't eat anything at lunch and Greg said you need to eat something. May I help you into the chair?"

Sherri pushed herself up on her elbows. Hannah looked Swedish, with beautiful skin and flaxen hair. She was tall, almost as tall as Greg. They made a nice-looking couple.

"Thank you. I'd appreciate it."

After they maneuvered her into the chair, Sherri pushed a button and it moved silently across the room. Hannah opened a door. "This is your bathroom. Will you need help?"

Not in this lifetime.

"I'm fine. Thank you."

She managed to get inside and closed the door. The room was about the size of her bedroom in the apartment. There was a free-standing shower and a large tub with jets. A long counter and mirror stretched across the width of the room.

Sherri had never been inside this particular bathroom. She found a washcloth and filled the sink with water. She bathed herself as well as she could. Somehow she would have to learn to help herself into the shower once her dressing came off. When the nurse changed it that morning, she had used a smaller dressing, saying that the incision looked healthy and was healing. There was a built-in seat inside the shower, plus shampoos, conditioners and creams. The place could have been a five-star hotel.

After struggling to get her clothes off, she wet a washcloth and washed herself with soapy water.

Sherri was drying off when she heard a tap on the door.

"Yes?"

Hannah said, "I've laid out your clothes for you. Greg will check in on you in about forty-five minutes."

Sherri finished drying herself and opened the door. She looked at the clothes laid out for her. They were new. She moved to the closet and opened the door. The walk-in closet had all of her clothes and several new things that still had tags on them.

She spun her chair around and crossed the room to the dresser. When she opened the drawers, she discovered all of her things were here…plus several new items.

He'd certainly been confident that she would fall in with his plans. Why not? He'd made certain that she had no place to go except here. She hated to admit that he'd been right about everything. She really couldn't have taken care of herself. What she had trouble understanding was why he'd do this for her. He'd put himself out to see that she had everything she needed, including Lucifer. Which was another thing. He'd once mentioned that he was allergic to cats. She'd been disappointed because she'd always loved them and once she settled into her apartment she had found the kittens. Thank goodness Joan had wanted one, too.

Now here they were, content to be nearby. It was difficult to be upset with him; he'd done so much for her at a time when she'd desperately needed help.

She took underwear out of the drawer and with a great deal of effort managed to get the pants over her cast. She was already exhausted. Hannah had laid out a simple pullover dress that was new. Sherri slipped it over her head. She pulled the sling over her shoulder and slipped her arm into it.

She was as ready as she would ever be. She saw no reason to wait for Greg. With new determination to be nicer to him, Sherri left the room.

Five

Out in the hallway, Sherri went back the way she and Greg had come into the house. She stopped at the French doors and admired the view. Greg had been given a truly wonderful gift. She knew he must miss Millie very much. Sherri wished she'd stayed in touch with her. As the minutes passed, she began to relax. It was difficult to believe that such a pastoral place existed only a few miles from downtown.

She was startled when Greg spoke behind her.

"Ah, there you are. Enjoying the view, I see."

She turned and faced him. "Thank you for all that you've done, Greg. I'm sorry that I've been so rude to you. It's just that—" She couldn't find the words to continue.

"I know. You'd made a clean break, and I was the last person you wanted in your life."

She nodded, looking down at her hands folded in her lap.

"Understood," he replied tersely. "I know how difficult all

of this is for you. I just want you to know that you have a place to stay here for as long as you want it."

She gave a quick shake of her head. "Don't you think having me here is unfair to Hannah?"

He looked puzzled. "Why should it be? One more person in the house isn't going to make much difference to her."

She almost rolled her eyes at his obtuseness. "In my opinion, having your wife looking after your ex-wife is asking a lot of her."

He made no effort to hide his amusement. "It certainly would be…if she were my wife. But then, she'd be a bigamist and I might have to arrest her." He turned her chair and they went to a small dining area not far from the kitchen. It was a cozy area with a bay window that brought the beauty of the lawn into the home.

"Hannah is happily married to Sven and I'm happy to have both of them living here. Actually, they live in the garage apartment, but that's close enough." He looked past her, flashing his heart-stopping smile. "Looks delicious, Hannah, as usual."

Sherri glanced around and saw the tray Hannah carried. Behind her, a large blond man carried two wineglasses and a bottle of wine.

"Sven," Greg said, "this is Sherri. She'll be staying here until she literally gets back on her feet. Sherri…Sven."

Sven's smile dazzled her with its brilliance. Unfortunately for her, she seemed to be immune to all men but Greg.

"Pleased to meet you."

"Sven is one of the best landscapers in the area. He has a thriving business, including a nursery not far from here. He takes care of this place, but refuses to take money for it." Greg smiled at Sven. "Not a good way to run a business, you know."

Sven shrugged. "It's only fair. You don't accept our rent payments."

"I definitely get the best of that deal."

While the two men talked, Hannah quickly placed the food on the table, lit the candles and refilled the water glasses.

Sherri looked at her food and sighed.

"Something wrong?"

"I see that I'm on a soft-food diet. I suppose this is better than clear liquids."

"The doctor said to keep you on a soft diet for another week. If you have no problems, you could have normal meals again. Believe me, once you taste Hannah's cooking you'll know it was worth waiting for."

She looked at his plate. Mmm. Baked chicken, mashed potatoes and what appeared to be fresh green beans. She almost whimpered with longing. Oh well. She picked up her soup spoon and began to eat. Actually, the food was delicious, much better than the hospital's food.

The room was so quiet she could hear the soft tick of a clock somewhere in the house. She needed to get away from Greg for her own emotional preservation. Right now, though, she intended to enjoy her meal and being in Millie's home once again.

Once she finished her meal, she said, "This was so good. My compliments to the chef."

Greg grinned. "My secret weapon to coax you into continuing to stay here."

She looked at him and he met her gaze. "I don't understand any of this, Greg. Yes, we used to be married. It didn't work. We've both moved on. Why in the world would you decide to take over my life like this?"

"Is that what it looks like to you?"

"That's what it is. I'm pretty much confined to this chair until my bones heal." She paused and said, "Did this chair belong to Millie?"

Greg nodded. "She fell last year and broke her hip."

"I can see her now, zipping around the place. She was really something."

"Yes, she was. I miss her a great deal."

"So, why am I here?" She came back to her question. "And don't answer a question with a question, okay?"

"I was hoping that we could use this time together as a chance to deal with some of the issues that caused the divorce."

She frowned. "You're looking for closure."

He nodded slowly. "Something like that. You moved out without any warning. You gave me no chance to deal with whatever was bothering you."

"Why don't we leave it at this—I left you because I discovered that I didn't really know you at all. What I did learn while we were married was that we were too different. We wanted different things in our lives. The longer I stayed, the more painful it was going to be to leave you. I also knew that if I talked to you about leaving, you would convince me to stay."

"I would have liked the chance to know what in the hell I did to make you leave like that and refuse to communicate with me except through your lawyer."

"Do you remember how we met and how quickly we came together?"

His lips quirked. "Oh, yeah. I remember it well." His gaze was so heated Sherri felt scorched.

"Granted we had a great sex life, but—"

"Better than great, Sherri. Much better."

"Okay. However, we didn't take time to get to know each

other out of bed. You wanted to spend our hours together in bed rather than talk to me."

"And your point is?"

She shook her head. "This discussion is pointless and I'm tired. You've been a wonderful support since the accident and I do appreciate it, but this isn't going to change anything between us, Greg. Being around you is upsetting, which is why I didn't want to talk to you once I left."

"You make me sound like an ogre."

"You're not." She looked around the room. "I can't believe we're having this conversation. I'm really tired. I think I'll go back to my room."

Greg sighed and then stood while she backed away from the table, turned and rolled away.

He followed her to her room. "You're going to need some help getting ready for bed."

As tired as she was, she knew he was right. "Perhaps Hannah could—"

"She and Sven are off-duty. There's no reason to have her come back when I'm here to help you."

She looked at him and thought about changing clothes in front of him. That would be all it would take to get them into bed together, surgery or not, broken bones or not. Why did he have to be so attractive? He made her motor run nonstop whenever he was around. Right now, she couldn't afford to be tempted.

"Don't worry about it. I changed my clothes without help earlier this evening."

"All right. At least let me put you on the bed before I leave."

She rolled to her dresser and found one of her sleep shirts before going to the bed. She held up her arms.

He picked her up as though she were weightless and sat her on the side of the bed.

"I'll see you in the morning," Greg said.

She nodded. He continued to stand there. She closed her eyes and looked down at her hands. She was on the verge of tears and she didn't want him to know. She was so vulnerable right now in so many ways. It would be so easy to forget what she'd gone through in their marriage and accept the here and now.

She'd tried to make a clean break but fate was against her. She heard Greg leave the room and quietly close the door behind him.

Greg poured himself another glass of wine and wandered out to the back terrace.

He'd always loved Millie. She had been agile, both mentally and physically, all of her life until her fall. He'd spent as much of his childhood as possible in this home. His brother had refused to come for more than a couple of days at a time, saying there was nothing to do here. Kyle had found it boring and had preferred to spend his summers in Connecticut with his friends.

Millie was the reason he'd moved to Austin directly after graduating from the Police Academy. He had visited her as often as he could. She was the family he'd never had, she and Sherri.

There was no way he could get Millie back but he was going to do everything in his power to have a second chance with Sherri. He loved her too much not to try, and tonight he'd realized that she wasn't indifferent to him.

That offered him a sliver of hope.

Six

Five years earlier

Greg Hogan saw the flashing lights from police cars and an ambulance before he turned into the restaurant's parking lot. The yellow police tape already encircled the area behind the place and forensics was there gathering evidence.

A man had been murdered and it was Greg's job to find his killer.

He pulled up alongside one of the police cars and walked over to the area.

"What have you got on the guy?" he asked one of the men, pulling a notebook out of his pocket.

"White male, forty-two years old, Kenneth Allred, according to one of his driver's licenses."

"What does the other one say?"

"He had four—Kenneth Allred, Fred Conway, Ken Crosley and Jerry Allen."

"Maybe his prints will be on file somewhere."

"We have an approximate time of death, based on a witness's statement."

Greg looked around the parking lot. "Has he been questioned yet?"

"She. She told us a little but she was so shaken that we placed her in a squad car with one of our men. We got the call forty-five minutes ago and were here in ten. One of the officers on patrol answered the call. The woman had gone back inside the restaurant and told the manager, who called it in."

"Did she see the murder?"

"She said she saw two men running to a car from behind the restaurant as she was getting into her car. Their car left and she backed out of her parking space and glanced behind the building. That's when she saw the victim." The policeman nodded toward the floodlights at the back of the building. "She was able to see that he was covered in blood. That's when she ran back inside."

"I'll talk to her…see if she can describe the men. I wonder if they saw her? Whatever else we do, we need to keep her name out of the papers in case they saw her and go looking for her."

Greg spent the next half hour studying the crime scene, discussing the findings with the forensic team and studying the body. When he was through, he walked over to the police car where the witness sat in the front seat, staring out the windshield. He nodded to the uniformed officer who immediately got out of the car. Greg slid inside and looked at the witness.

The first thing he noticed was how small she was. She had thick, dark hair that tumbled around her shoulders.

"Ms. Masterson?" he said softly.

As though she were in a daze, she slowly turned to look at him.

"Yes?"

He held his hand out to her. "I'm Detective Greg Hogan." She hesitantly offered her hand to him. He wasn't surprised to find it cold. "Would you like to go inside and have a cup of coffee?"

Her husky voice intrigued him. She looked like a teenager and yet sounded like a seductive woman. "All right."

He walked around the car and helped her out. She was shaking. Scenes like these were rough on civilians.

The manager had closed the restaurant. When he saw Greg at the door, he came over and let them inside.

"Hi. I'm Randy Kramer," he said, offering his hand to Greg.

Greg shook his hand and replied, "Detective Greg Hogan, Homicide. Could we have some coffee, please?"

"Certainly. I've been sending coffee out to the men since they arrived."

Greg led her to one of the booths. After she slid in, he sat opposite her.

Under the lights, he could see that her eyes were green and she had the longest lashes he'd ever seen.

"I have some questions for you. I know you've already talked to one of the policemen. I just have some follow-up questions for you if that's okay."

Randy placed two mugs of coffee in front of them. The woman immediately wrapped her fingers around the steaming cup.

Finally, she nodded at him.

"Okay. Let's start with your name and address."

"Sherri Masterson. The address is 2610 Mockingbird Lane."

"Are you employed?"

"I'm finishing my last semester at the university. I help out on weekends at a pet store whenever I can."

"How old are you?"

"Twenty-one."

Greg concentrated on getting all of this on paper, but it was tough. He was having such a strong reaction to the woman…girl…that he was embarrassed. He had never met a woman who affected him so suddenly. Maybe he'd been working too many hours or hadn't been with a woman for too long, but something was going on that was interfering with his concentration.

He cleared his throat. "Let's go back a few hours and describe what you were doing."

"They needed me to fill in this afternoon at the pet store for an employee who'd gone home sick. After my eleven o'clock class I went in and worked the rest of the day. A friend called me and asked me to go out. We met and had dinner."

"Was he with you when you left?"

"No. He'd parked in front. He watched as I crossed the parking lot and waved when I reached my car."

"Did he see the two men?"

She swallowed. "I don't know."

"Okay. So you got in your car. Then what?"

"I dropped my keys and they fell beneath the car. I had to reach under the car a little to get them. When I stood, I saw those two men running to a car parked in back."

"Did you happen to notice the make or model of the car?"

She was already shaking her head before he finished the question. "I'm sorry, but I don't know much about cars. It was either dark blue or black." She closed her eyes for a moment. Then she looked at him. "I think it had four doors."

"Texas plates?"

"I didn't notice. Seeing two men hurrying to a car didn't set off any alarms for me. I figured they were late for something."

"Okay. Then what happened?"

"When they backed out, their headlights blinded me. I couldn't make out anything at all. Then they gunned the car and sped away."

"What did you do then?"

"I got into my car and pulled out, preparing to drive away. When I glanced around to make sure there were no other cars, I happened to see—" she swallowed again "—this, uh, this man and he was, uh, he was sprawled near the back door of the restaurant. The way he lay, and the sight of so much blood, made me think he was dead."

"So you came inside?"

"Yes. I told the manager, who called 911."

Greg leaned back in the booth and Sherri lifted her cup to her mouth, using both hands. She swallowed some coffee and carefully put the cup down.

"I know this is difficult for you." He looked at his notes deliberately so he wouldn't see the vulnerability in her eyes. It was all he could do not to move to the other side of the booth and put his arm around her for comfort. "Did you hear anyone say anything?"

"No."

"Were you in your car or still standing beside it when their lights blinded you?"

"I was standing beside it."

Which meant that they would be able to identify her. Great. Just great.

"Okay. I'd appreciate it if you could describe these men to

me…whatever you can remember. Were they tall or short, thin or heavy, move with a limp, anything like that?"

She clasped her hands and was silent for a moment. Finally, she shook her head. "I'm sorry. I know I'm not being very helpful, but I didn't see their faces. I really didn't pay much attention to them."

"But you did see them run. Long strides? Short strides? Athletic? Or laboring?"

"Oh. Well, I would say they were both agile. They practically sprinted. They were both tall, at least to me, but then everyone is tall to me."

"Can you guess a height?"

"Mmm. Maybe five ten, five eleven. How tall are you?"

He was startled by her question. "Six one."

"I guessed six feet, so I think I'm fairly accurate on their heights."

"Would you please give me the name of your friend, just in case he may have seen them?"

"Sure." She gave Greg the name and phone number.

"All right. If you don't mind coming to the station in the morning I'd like to show you some mug shots as well as get your written statement. I don't think it will take long."

"Okay."

They stood and he escorted her to her car. "I'd like to follow you home, if you don't mind. I'm somewhat concerned that the men you saw may start looking for you. Let's keep you as safe as possible."

"I'm all for that."

He walked her to her car, noting that the ambulance and the uniforms were gone. Only the yellow tape remained.

Greg waited until Sherri pulled out and headed toward the street and then he pulled in behind her. Once they reached her apartment building, he watched her until she disappeared inside, giving him a little wave as she did.

He needed to get his notes into the computer and get to work.

Sherri hurried into her apartment, closed and locked the door and turned on every light in the place. Then she went into the bathroom and threw up. After she washed her face and rinsed out her mouth, she went into her minuscule kitchen and got out a small carton of yogurt.

She turned out the living room/dining room/kitchen light and went to her bedroom. She glanced at her watch. It was eleven o'clock. She felt as though she'd been up all night. She sat on the side of her bed and finished her yogurt. Then she went in and took a long, warm shower.

When she finally crawled into bed and turned out the light her mind returned to the dead man. She shivered. She hadn't gone near him but she had seen what he looked like from her car.

Sherri wished she could remember more about those men. They had definitely got a good look at her. Would they think she could identify them? She sincerely hoped not.

When Sherri drifted off to sleep she didn't dream about the murder. Instead she dreamed about Detective Greg Hogan of Homicide.

In her dream something or someone was chasing her. She was in a panic because she couldn't get away. Next, Greg Hogan was there. She ran into his arms, knowing she'd be safe. He held her so close she could hear and feel his heart beating. In the next scene she was watching him slowly take off his clothes…baring his broad shoulders and muscled chest, slowly unfastening his pants and sliding them down.

She was mesmerized by his male beauty. He held out his hand and she took it, only then aware that she was nude.

He held her close and began to kiss her, which kindled flames of longing in her. He laid her on a wide bed and continued to kiss her as his hand stroked her body. She returned his kisses, feverishly wanting him to make love to her.

Sherri looked into his eyes as he moved away slightly and settled between her legs. Yes! This was what she wanted! She—

She woke up with a start. What in the world? She'd been dreaming about that detective. She sat up in bed and clutched her head. The dream had been so real.

How embarrassing. She had to go to the police station this morning to look at photos and to write out her statement. How was she going to be able to face him after having had such an erotic dream about him? How strange. Why would she have dreamed such a dream? She'd barely noticed him last night.

Liar. You were scared but not so scared that you missed his strong features, his sensuous mouth and his gentleness with you.

She went into the bathroom and took her shower, adjusting the water to be cooler than normal.

Seven

"Hey, Hogan, you've got a visitor."

Greg looked up from the file he was working on and saw Sherri Masterson standing just inside the bull pen area of the station, looking a little lost. He stood, once again irritated by his body's instant reaction to her.

Today she wore some kind of flowery dress. Greg forced himself to concentrate on why she was here while he strode over to where she waited.

Greg stuck out his hand, "Mornin', Ms. Masterson. Thank you for coming in. I know last night was very traumatic for you. Did you sleep well?"

His innocent question caused her to turn a fascinating red and she looked away from him. Now what was that about? Had she spent the night with her boyfriend? He didn't know why, but that thought bothered him.

"Mmm, yes, I slept all right…and please call me Sherri."

"Sure. And I'm Greg." He took her elbow and felt her stiffen. He immediately stepped away. "I've set up one of the rooms for us so we can have some privacy."

And she blushed again. What was her problem? He tried not to come across as intimidating, but she was definitely nervous around him.

He cleared his throat. "Would you like some coffee?"

She smiled. "Is it as bad as I've heard police station coffee generally is?"

He grinned. "Naw. We just want people to think that. Otherwise, we'd take most of Starbucks' business away."

She chuckled and he relaxed a little. Maybe this wasn't going to be as bad as he'd feared. His biggest concern was that she might be picking up his strong attraction to her. He was a professional and he didn't want anything to get in the way of obtaining this woman's help in solving a murder.

"Yes, thank you. I'll take some coffee."

He opened a door and motioned to the table. "Have a seat and I'll be right back."

He closed the door behind him and took a big breath. He was being absolutely ridiculous. Maybe he should get his partner to do the interview. No, that wouldn't work because he would somehow have to explain why he couldn't do it.

He poured two mugs of coffee and headed back to the interview room.

"Here you are," he said, setting one of the mugs in front of her and sitting down across the table. "I'd like you to write out your statement for me. If anything came to mind since we spoke, please let me know."

She sipped her coffee. "Okay."

He watched her write. She was a lefty. When she finally

looked up, she caught him staring at her. He quickly blinked and smiled.

"Finished?"

"I think so. I can't think of anything else."

She handed him the paper and he put it aside. He opened a file and pulled out a photograph. "Have you ever seen this man before?"

Sherri took the picture and studied it. This wasn't a mug shot. The man was smiling into the camera, his arms around two small children.

She looked up. "You know, I think he may have been in the restaurant last night."

"Really?"

"I wouldn't swear to it, but his smile reminds me of a man we passed as the hostess led us to a table. In fact, my friend teased me about it." She looked back down. "I didn't pay all that much attention to him, though. He left before we did. Is he important to this case?"

"He's the victim in this case."

"Oh, no!" She sounded horrified. "Are you sure?"

He nodded. "I spoke with his family this morning and they gave me this photograph."

"Are these his children?"

"One is. The other one is his nephew. We wanted to see if he'd been in the restaurant that night. His wife said he had a meeting to go to, although he didn't say where."

"I'm so sorry for his family."

"Was he alone when you saw him?"

She thought about his question before finally saying, "He was when we passed him. After that I had my back to him. All I know was that he wasn't there when we passed that table on the way out."

"We interviewed several people, including your friend, who were at the restaurant last night. You seem to be the only person who actually saw the two men run from behind the restaurant."

She shivered.

He moved his hand so that it rested on hers. "They have no idea who you are. You don't have anything to worry about."

She looked at his hand. He noted that his hand swallowed hers. She didn't pull away so he left it there. She looked back at him. "But they saw me very clearly. They saw my car."

"Unless they have someone in their pocket who can run a DMV check on you, they won't bother you."

She nodded. "Okay."

"Next, I'd like you to look at some of these mug shots to see if you recognize anyone. We're still investigating his possible contacts and hoping you see someone here that you recognize."

He opened the book and she blinked. "That's a lot of people. And I never saw their faces."

"There may be something that might trigger a memory…a tilt of a head, the shape of a jaw, that sort of thing. I'll leave you to look and will be back a little later."

He checked on her from time to time, but in the end she didn't recognize anyone.

"I'm so sorry. I know I'm not being much help," she said.

"Actually, you are. We know these guys weren't involved."

"We can hope. I should have been more aware."

Greg looked at his watch. "It's almost lunchtime. Would you care to go get something to eat? That is, if you don't have other plans."

She stood and stretched, causing her top to ride up and bare her midriff. Greg looked away but he was too late to stop his reaction to the sight. He had a sudden desire to kiss her right there.

"Actually, lunch sounds good. I sort of skipped breakfast this morning."

"Great." He opened the door and ushered her out of the room.

He drove them to one of the cafés where he generally ate lunch. It was a little hole-in-the-wall place that served the best hamburgers in town.

Once inside and seated, Sherri looked around the room in wonder. "I never knew this place was here."

He grinned. "Another top secret among law-enforcement guys. They're open all the time and there have been times when it was the only place where we could get something to eat."

"Do they have trouble with people dealing drugs late at night? I've heard that the places that stay open all night tend to attract them."

"No. They've made it clear to the people who come in that the place is frequented by off-duty as well as on-duty cops. Seems to work."

Once they gave their order, Greg leaned on his folded arms and asked, "Tell me a little about yourself."

She looked at him in surprise, obviously startled by the question. "Didn't you get all that information from me last night?"

He grinned. "This isn't about the case, Sherri. I've tried my darnedest to hide the fact that I'm attracted to you but I can't seem to be detached where you're concerned. This is just for my own information."

Her cheeks flamed. "Oh."

He lifted his shoulder in a shrug. "Of course, it may be all one-sided, so if you'd rather not—"

"Uh, no. It isn't at all one-sided."

He settled back in the booth with a grin and said, "Good. Let's hear it."

"My life is very ordinary. I've been in school most of my life, it seems. Right now I'm taking a course in computer software and technical writing."

"How about family?"

She shook her head. "No family. Parents died when I was fourteen. The aunt who took over caring for me died of cancer last year."

"You've had some tough breaks."

"Since I can't do anything about the past, I do my best to look forward to the future."

Their food arrived and they concentrated on their meal. Once they finished, Sherri looked at him and said, "Your turn."

He looked at her quizzically for a moment and then nodded. "What do you want to know?"

"How old you are…are you married…what about family? Those things. Oh, and why you decided to go into law enforcement."

"Are you sure you aren't writing my biography?"

"Depends on how interesting it might be."

"Oh. In that case, you'll be bored right away, so I'm safe."

He paused. He didn't like talking about himself. Hated it, in fact. However, if he wanted to spend time with Sherri…which he definitely did…he'd better give her some idea of who he was.

"Let's see. I'm twenty-seven years old, never been married, got a degree and immediately went into the Police Academy."

"Did you go to college here in Austin?"

Okay, no hedging. "Actually I, uh, no, I didn't. I graduated from Harvard."

Her eyebrows went up. "Really?"

"Yep."

"Are you originally from the East Coast?"

"I have to admit I'm not a native Texan, but I got here as soon as I could."

She laughed, which was what he wanted. "Have you traveled much during those twenty-seven years?"

"Some," he replied.

"What made you come to Texas?"

"Because my great-grandmother lives here."

"So what made you want to be a detective?"

"You know, there are times when I've wondered about that, myself. I guess I like the idea of being on the side of the good guys. I like challenges, solving puzzles, that sort of thing." He glanced at his watch and said, "Which reminds me that I need to get back to work."

They slipped out of the booth and he took her hand as though it was the most natural thing in the world. *Uh-oh, Hogan, better slow down.*

He paid for their lunch and they went outside. "I've got to admit, I'd rather run and play."

She glanced up at him and stole his breath away. He'd never been so strongly attracted to anyone. What was going on with him, anyway?

They drove back to the station in silence. Once there, he walked her to her car. He opened the door and said, "I'd like to see you again, Sherri."

Her green eyes sparkled. "I'd like that."

"Okay, how about next Friday? We can grab a bite to eat, maybe catch a movie if you'd like." And he would do his best not to seduce her. Unless, of course, she wanted him to.

"That sounds like fun."

He leaned down and gave her a chaste kiss. Anyway, it was supposed to be chaste, but when she responded so beautifully he might have lingered a little longer than he had intended. He straightened and placed his hands behind his back. At least he hadn't grabbed her.

She got into her car. "Friday, then."

"Around seven."

"See you."

He watched her drive away and already felt the loss of her company. Oh, brother, he had it bad. He'd known her less than twenty-four hours and he didn't want to let her out of his sight. Ever.

Eight

Sherri really didn't need the car on her way home. She could have floated there.

Greg Hogan had kissed her! He was practically a stranger and he wasn't one to talk about himself much, so she really didn't know much about him. Common sense told her that she needed to get to know him better before feeling so swept away by him.

She'd never responded to anyone the way she had to Greg. Of course, it could be a result of her dream. She certainly felt she knew him much better than she actually did. She got hot just remembering the dream.

What should she do? She'd said yes to seeing him again, but was that wise? She thought about it for a while until she came to a conclusion: she had no idea. All she knew was that she didn't intend to cancel their date.

He'd graduated from Harvard? He'd chosen police work

for a career? Greg Hogan was definitely a complex man…and so very fascinating, as well.

Once home, she forced herself to think about the homework she needed to finish before Monday. She was scheduled to work at the pet store this afternoon and tomorrow afternoon. Her plans had been to study after dinner last night, but her study schedule had been abandoned while she dealt with the horror of what she'd seen.

Once she got home, she immediately focused on her schoolwork. All week she could enjoy the anticipation of knowing that she would see Greg next Friday.

She began to hum as she opened one of her books.

He tapped on her apartment door the next Friday at seven o'clock. Sherri hurried to let him inside. She'd had a crisis when it came to deciding what to wear. She didn't want to dress too sexily in case he got the wrong idea about her. However, she did want to look attractive.

She was a little short on date clothes. She spent her time on campus hanging out with other students and had never worried about what she looked like.

Tonight she did.

She opened the door and her knees went weak. He grinned at her. She fought to regain some composure. "Please come inside."

He wore a sports jacket over a pair of khakis. The jacket looked custom-made and he looked delectable. She wanted to throw herself into his arms and dramatically cry, "Take me, take me. I'm all yours!"

He stepped inside her apartment and looked around. "I like what you've done with the place."

She looked at it more objectively and said, "Goodwill stuff, mostly."

"Did you do the refinishing on this table?" He rubbed his thumb along the surface. She was rather proud of that one.

"I've refinished and reupholstered most of the furniture I own."

He turned and looked at her. "You're quite talented."

She swallowed. "Thanks." Seen through his eyes, the place must look like a typical college girl's room, with the big colorful posters and some watercolors she'd painted once for a class. He was very much a sophisticated man about town, while she felt awkward and flustered.

He glanced at his watch and said, "Ready to go?"

Without a word she picked up her purse and turned to the door.

"How long have you lived here?" he asked, helping her into his car.

"Since I was a freshman. I preferred to get a smaller place that I could afford rather than have a roommate."

Sherri finally began to relax with Greg during dinner. He entertained her with various stories, all amusing, about work and his coworkers, but she idly noted that he didn't talk about himself at all.

They did compare their favorite movies and musicians and laughed about how diverse their tastes were. He liked thrillers and war movies while she preferred something light, like romantic comedies. However, the movie they decided to see was one she'd heard a lot about, and she was more than willing to see it with him.

"Just don't be surprised if I suddenly hide my face in your shoulder."

"Don't worry. I'll put my arm around you so you'll know you're safe."

Her dream popped up in her head and she recalled that she had run to him in her dream and felt safe in his arms. She felt she could trust this man who was more stranger than friend. It seemed almost as though she'd known him from somewhere long ago—a past life or something—and they had found each other again.

Sherri didn't dare say any of that to him; he'd think she was crazy. At the moment she couldn't swear that she wasn't a little insane to think they might have known each other before now.

They got popcorn and drinks and went inside the theatre. Sherri noticed that Greg caught every female's eye from little girls to octogenarians. She could certainly relate.

The movie was excellent, a thriller with one of her favorite actors in it. Greg had placed his arm around her when the movie started.

Once the movie was over, they left the theatre hand in hand and strolled back to his car.

"Would you like to stop somewhere for coffee?" he asked.

Okay. She'd been practicing and hoped she sounded casual when she answered, "Why don't we go to my place? I'll make coffee and I've got some bakery cookies if you want something more than coffee."

"I'm not going to touch that one," he replied wryly.

She laughed.

They pulled up in front of her apartment building and climbed the stairs to the second story. Greg was teasing her about staying in shape because of the climb when he came to an abrupt stop and grabbed her wrist.

She looked at him in alarm. "What?"

He nodded toward her door. She hadn't noticed that the door of her apartment was slightly ajar until he pointed it out. She froze. He put his finger to his lips and pulled her behind him.

She had no idea when he'd pulled a pistol. She didn't even know he carried one but there was one in his hand now.

"Stay here," he said next to her ear.

She nodded.

He moved closer and listened. After several moments he pushed the door open and waited.

Nothing happened.

Greg found the light switch just inside the door and flipped it on. She peered around the door and gasped.

"I told you to stay back there," he said gruffly. "I need to check out the rest of the place."

She nodded mutely, her fist to her mouth.

Someone had come in and destroyed her apartment. There was no other word to describe it. Every piece of furniture had been broken or ripped apart. Curtains hung in shreds, dishes were smashed and when she followed Greg into her bedroom, she saw that her closet had been emptied and her clothes ripped into pieces. She didn't need to check her drawers because they were broken and on the floor, their contents cut up.

Her bed had fared no better. Mattress stuffing littered the bed and floor, along with the remains of her pillows and linens.

Without a word Sherri stepped around Greg, who had put his gun away, and stepped inside her bathroom.

"Be careful," he said from behind her. "Shattered glass and pieces of the mirror are on the floor."

She didn't want to see any more. Sherri turned away and saw Greg using his cell phone.

"Get the forensic team over here now." He rattled off her address and hung up before looking at her. "We'll wait outside until they get here. I don't want to contaminate the scene."

Sherri looked around her. She felt violated. Someone had broken into her apartment and deliberately and systematically destroyed it. She had nothing left: no clothes, no place to sleep, nothing. The whole apartment had been defiled. She wrapped her arms around her waist and shivered.

Greg touched her shoulder. "They'll be here in a few minutes. Let's get some air."

Only then did Sherri notice the heavy scent of cologne from the broken bottles in the bathroom. Once out in the hallway he pulled her close to his side and continued to hold her as they walked outside and back to his car.

He opened her door and waited for her to slide inside the car before he carefully closed it and walked around to the other side.

The man who had taken her to dinner and a movie was gone. In his place was a frowning, tough and formidable cop.

Greg got into the car and turned toward her. "I would say that someone left you a very strong message."

She returned his gaze, her eyes dry. "I think I got that. It looks like every Friday is the thirteenth to me."

"Do you have any idea who might have done this? A former boyfriend, a jealous female?"

"I have no former boyfriend and if anyone is jealous of me, that's news to me. "

He took her hand and she saw a flash of the Greg with whom she'd spent the evening. "I'm so sorry you have to go through this."

She looked down at their clasped hands. "Me, too. It really is a bit much. Everything I own is destroyed as though a fire had swept through. Nothing is salvageable. The only clothes I have at the moment are what I'm wearing."

"I know. We'll deal with that a little later."

A couple of cruisers arrived and Greg got out of his car. He walked over and spoke to the driver of one of them. Two others got out of the second car and joined him. She recognized one of them whom she'd seen last week investigating the murder.

She shivered. What if— No, she didn't want to go there.

After several minutes the two men and a woman followed Greg back into the apartment building.

How did whoever had done this know she'd be gone this evening? Was she being watched? She glanced around the parking lot and quickly locked the doors.

Greg returned shortly and she unobtrusively unlocked the doors.

He got into the car and started the engine. Once out of the parking lot he headed away from the university area.

"Where are we going?"

"I'm taking you home with me," he said softly. "You'll be safe there, I promise you that. You can use my other bedroom until we get all of this settled."

She had no intention of arguing with him. "There is one thing," she finally said.

"Yes?"

"I need to stop at a store and get a few things."

"We can do that." He changed lanes and signaled to turn left. After a few miles, he turned into the parking lot of a large store that stayed open late.

There were few cars around. Not too many shoppers at close to midnight on a Friday night.

Greg parked across from the entrance and stopped.

"Thank you. I won't be long."

"Doesn't matter. I'm coming with you."

"Oh, that isn't—"

"Yes, it is. We're going to be joined at the hip until this thing is put to rest."

"You think it has something to do with the murder," she stated, suddenly feeling exhausted.

"That's one of the theories I'm working on. We hope to find some prints in that mess. If not, we'll continue to follow other leads. I don't want to take any chances where you're concerned. The men you saw could very well believe that you saw them and reported it."

"So they've been watching me?"

He nodded. "Has anything unusual happened to you this week? Besides your apartment being destroyed, I mean."

"Well, I don't know how unusual it is, but I've gotten several hang-up calls. Probably wrong numbers."

"Or checking if you're home."

She stared at him in surprise. "I suppose."

"My guess is that they're trying to scare you."

"They have definitely done that."

He groaned. "And I've made it worse by showing an interest in you. They think you're giving me additional information."

"That's a logical assumption."

"But we both know that isn't the reason I asked you out."

She bit her bottom lip. She refused to cry in front of him, but it was tough because he was being nice to her. It had been easier to hide her emotions when he was in his cop mode.

"Let's go shopping," he said, opening his door. She got out and met him in front of his car.

"From now on, you wait until I open your door."

"I've been opening my own doors for years. I'm sure I can handle it."

"So if a car happened to pull up beside you as you were getting out of the car, and a couple of men grabbed you and threw you into the back of their car…or van…you could cope with that?"

"Are you trying to scare mè?"

"If it makes you a little less independent for a while."

"I've never been the damsel-in-distress type."

He took her elbow and guided her across toward the front of the store. "We'll have to do something about that."

Nine

Greg lived in a quiet, residential area, made up of several apartment buildings that looked so much alike Sherri wondered how anyone would know which one was his or hers.

He pulled into a covered parking area. "We'll get your car in the morning. I have two parking spaces."

Sherri had so little energy left she had to force herself to get out of the car and gather the sacks in the backseat that contained all of her worldly belongings.

Greg gathered the ones she couldn't reach from her side and, once the doors were closed, locked the car. Without a word, he led her across the driveway to one of the buildings, climbed two stories to the top floor and strode to the door of one of the apartments.

"Talk about getting your exercise," Sherri said in a strained voice.

"I like it up here." He opened the door and waved her

inside. Once he had turned the light on, Sherri looked around. The apartment was much larger than hers and had a nice view of the hills west of Austin.

However, the place was definitely a bachelor's pad. Newspapers were scattered around on tables and the floor, a pair of sneakers sat beneath the coffee table, a few dishes sat on the kitchen counter and more were in the sink.

"I could make excuses for the way the place looks," Greg said. He must have noticed her looking around. "But the truth is, this is cleaner…and less cluttered…than usual."

He continued toward the hallway and she followed him. He stopped midway and opened the door to a bedroom. "I'll get some sheets and stuff." He pointed to the door opposite. "That's the bathroom. It's yours. I have one off my bedroom."

Sherri walked into the room and looked around. The bed had no headboard, but there was a bedside table and a chest of drawers.

"I'm not sure what's in the closet, but whatever's there, shove it aside."

She turned and looked at him. "I doubt that I'll need much space." She laid the sacks on the bed. He dropped his beside hers and put his arms around her. He rocked her gently and after a moment she slipped her arms around his waist.

Sherri had no idea how long they stood there. When he eventually let go of her, all he said was, "I'll get the bedding for you."

While he was gone, she hung up the few clothes she'd bought, placed her underwear and a couple of sleep shirts in a drawer and took her toiletries across the hall to the bathroom.

When she came out she almost collided with Greg.

"Sorry," she said.

"No problem." He made short work of making the bed with her help.

He glanced over the room before looking at her. "If you need anything, just let me know."

She nodded.

"Good night," he said and closed the door behind him. He had turned on the lamp beside the bed when they'd first walked in and now it was her only source of light.

By now, she was too tired to think straight. She got her sleepwear out of the drawer and went across the hall. A warm shower helped to revive her a little. Once she'd brushed her teeth, Sherri stumbled back to her room, closed the door, turned off the light and dropped onto the bed.

The smell of freshly brewed coffee woke Sherri the next morning. She glanced at the clock and saw that it was almost ten. She didn't think she'd moved all night.

She quickly dressed and visited her bathroom. When she came out, she followed the scent of coffee.

Greg sat at the counter reading the paper, but looked up immediately when she walked into the room. She'd made no sound that she knew of. He wore battered jeans that clung to him like a second skin and an old sweatshirt with the arms cut out of it. The outfit on anyone else would look ratty. On him, it was sexy as all get-out.

"Mornin'," he said. "Ready for coffee?"

"More than ready," she replied, still standing in the hall doorway. "I didn't mean to sleep this late."

"You obviously needed it. Shock works that way on people sometimes and you've definitely had your share of that during the past week." He poured her a mug of coffee from the carafe by his elbow.

Sherri walked across the room and slipped onto the bar stool next to him, feeling his body heat beside her. She shivered and picked up the cup of coffee, inhaling the tantalizing scent.

"I'm afraid I don't have much here for breakfast…or any other meal, unless you have an addiction to sandwiches. I thought we could go out a little later for breakfast…or lunch…and maybe do some grocery shopping."

"Okay," she said softly.

They sat there in companionable silence. He offered her a piece of the newspaper and she took it.

When they were finished with the paper and coffee, Sherri asked, "How did those men find me?"

"A good question. We're looking for an answer to that."

"Did they think I'd leave town after last night?"

"At the very least, they were hoping to frighten you."

"Then their plan worked. Just thinking about what they did to my place gives me the creeps. I don't understand people like that. The destruction was so brutal and personal. Why would they destroy my clothes?"

Greg shook his head. "Once we know who did it, we'll find out why it was done."

"So you think you'll be able to find out who they were?"

"Generally speaking, people hired to do that kind of de-struction aren't the sharpest blades in the drawer. Even if they wore plastic gloves there's a chance we can pick up a shoe print. There's always evidence to be found when we sift through everything. There's no need for you to be frightened. You'll be safe here."

She nodded and tried not to look at him. How was she going to make herself immune to his presence? She was already at-tracted to him more than she'd ever been to any man. Seeing him the last thing at night and the first thing in the morning, could become addictive and would play havoc with her peace of mind.

"So what next?" she asked after a long silence.

He looked at her and smiled. "What do you usually do on Saturdays?"

"Clean house, go shopping, pay bills, study." She shrugged. "I guess I don't need to worry about cleaning."

He laughed. "If you're afraid you'll get out of practice, you can always do something around here."

She glanced around the room before meeting his gaze. The teasing glint in his eyes was adorable.

"Ah, now I get it. I pay for my room by keeping the place clean, right?" She couldn't hide the amusement in her voice.

He sobered. "No, of course not. There are no strings attached to my offer, I promise."

"I have a hunch I'll get in plenty of practice getting my apartment cleared out and cleaned up."'

"I hired a crew to go in and clean up the place and told the owner about what had happened. He agreed to let you out of your lease, given the circumstances."

"You've already done that this morning?"

"Yes. I also had one of the men tow your car over here. I didn't want it sitting over there any longer than necessary."

"I'm not helpless, you know," she said, feeling exasperated. "I'm perfectly capable of cleaning my apartment and of retrieving my own car."

"Okay. Sorry. I wanted to save you some of the grief. If you want to keep the apartment, you can let the manager know before he rents it out again."

She closed her eyes and rubbed her forehead. "I haven't thought that far ahead. I would have liked to at least save anything that was salvageable."

"The cleaners figured as much and will see what is fixable,

which they will save, and what isn't worth trying to put back together will get tossed."

"There's really nothing worth anything, even when it was whole."

As though unaware of what he was doing, Greg placed his hand at the back of her neck and massaged the bunched muscles there. The relief was immediate.

"Why don't we go get something to eat," he said after a while. "We both need some fuel."

"I think you're right. I'll need to go to the library afterwards. I need to replace some of the textbooks that were damaged so I can finish up my assignments." She got up and walked over to the window. When she turned around, she said, "I appreciate your offer of a place to stay more than I can say. You were right. I don't want to stay in that apartment, and your talking to the landlord in your official capacity no doubt saved me a great deal of hassle.

"I need to find my own place, though. I'll check the newspapers and see what I can find. You've been such a help and I don't want to take advantage of your kindness."

"Of course the decision is up to you. I have no problem with having you here. Until we get to the bottom of all of this, I'm a little worried about your living by yourself. If they found you so quickly once, they won't have any trouble finding where you've moved."

She allowed herself a small smile. "If they trace me here, they're going to wish they'd never bothered me."

He stood and stretched. "I almost wish they would. I'm getting hungry. Shall we go?"

"Let me get my purse." She hurried down the hall and into her bedroom. Tears filled her eyes. What would she have done without Greg these past several hours? He had stepped in and done what needed to be done.

She hadn't had anyone help her that much in years. The longer she stayed with him, the more susceptible she would become. Let's face it. She was already halfway in love with him.

Sherri grabbed a tissue and quickly wiped her eyes, checked her hair and lipstick, grabbed her purse and returned to the living room.

Greg had changed shirts. Now he wore a crisp, white T-shirt that set off his tan. He really was something.

She smiled and said, "I'm ready."

He stood by the bar, and when he saw her he picked up a key that had been lying on the counter. "I meant to give you this sooner. It's the key to the apartment. Since we're splitting up after breakfast, I want you to have a way to get in just in case I don't get here before you return."

"Thank you."

"I'd like you to keep very aware of your surroundings, including any cars that keep showing up wherever you happen to be. Watch the people around you, especially their eyes. Eyes generally telegraph what people plan to do. Key my cell phone number into your phone so that you can get me by a push of a button."

He put his hands on her shoulders and looked into her eyes. "I want you to be as safe as possible."

"I'll certainly do my best."

He draped his arm around her shoulders. "Good. Let's go eat."

Once inside the car, Greg reviewed what he'd done and said.

Meeting Sherri had been like being hit by a bolt of lightning. He'd been feeling and acting strange ever since then. Why else would he have brought her to his apartment?

He had never offered to share his apartment with anyone, no matter how desperate they happened to be. He liked his own space. He'd lived alone for a long time.

There was no reason why he couldn't have paid for a hotel for Sherri last night. He could have taken her to her room and made certain the room was safe before leaving her.

However, this morning he'd awakened with relief at the knowledge that he knew for certain she was safe because she was just down the hall from him.

He wished he knew why this particular woman had turned his life upside down and sideways. He had the insane desire to grab her and hold her and protect her from any possible harm. How unprofessional was that?

Then again, last night he'd been off duty and on a date with a delightful woman who took his breath away every time she flashed those green eyes at him. Even if the break-in had something to do with his case, he'd been first and foremost her companion last night.

What he had to do was to solve the murder. After that, his interest in her would in no way be professional.

His fear of getting involved with anyone had been overcome by the need to see Sherri as often as possible. He was now in unfamiliar territory because he'd never felt so strongly about anyone before now.

He'd didn't care for the vulnerability his feelings caused, but leaving her out of his life at this point would be impossible.

Ten

Ten days later Sherri let herself into Greg's apartment. She was relieved that he wasn't there. Of course, everything about the place reminded her of him but, when he was there, his force field pulled her to him like a magnet.

The only way she'd learned to deal with the tension between them was to spend as little time around him as possible. When they were in the apartment at the same time, he never came close to her, which was good, actually. If he'd ever touched her, she would probably have leaped on him and begged him to make love to her.

She had enough problems at the moment. She certainly didn't need to fall in love with her temporary roommate.

Too late. Way too late.

"Oh, shut up," she told herself. "It's just the situation. I'd feel the same way about any man I lived with under these circumstances."

Liar, liar, pants on fire.

"Would you please just shut up?"

Well, she was doing something about it. She planned to go apartment-hunting tomorrow. She'd finished her finals, thank goodness, and graduation was only a few weeks away. Hallelujah.

She had no reason to stay in Austin after that. She was as free as a bird. She could move anywhere she wanted. She could find a job somewhere else, although one of her teachers had mentioned that he'd had inquiries regarding the need for entry-level technical writers and he had recommended her to a couple of companies.

Didn't matter. She'd be much better off going somewhere new where there wouldn't be a chance of running into Greg.

They had reached a compromise after that first day. She would follow her routine during the day, but if she went anywhere at night, he would accompany her.

He'd suggested a movie tonight to celebrate the end of her finals. Not that she'd mentioned that she was taking them these past few days. Of course, it would be rudimentary detective work to figure out that she was doing a lot of studying, preparing papers and psyching herself up for the exams.

So. What the heck. They would grab a bite to eat and see a comedy. They would be coming full circle from the first date. A nice way to end things.

You are so full of it. You can't be serious.

She grabbed two handfuls of hair and tugged on them, trying not to scream with frustration…with the stupid voice in her head, with her not-so-secret longing for Greg and, to make matters worse, her steadily growing sexual frustration.

Seeing him every day, smelling the scent of his bath soap, his aftershave, even his toothpaste, kept her motor running.

She almost hummed with sexual tension. She saw him first thing in the morning and the last thing at night. Any red-blooded female living with a great-looking, charming and extremely sexy male would be frustrated.

He certainly wasn't bothered about being around *her.* He was engrossed in his cases. After all, hers wasn't the only one on his plate. Up until now, her studying had kept her busy. She wasn't certain what she would do with herself now. Get a job? Hunt for an apartment?

Everywhere she turned, it seemed, she was reminded of her feelings for Greg: If she did any reading…a romantic novel, or a suspense novel with some romance thrown in, or watched a drama on television that included love scenes, she pictured Greg in the leading man's role. When she saw couples on campus walking hand in hand, or with their arms around each other or kissing, she had the strongest impulse to yell, "Get a room!" at them. She needed no reminders, thank you very much.

Envy was not a pretty thing.

Yes. It was definitely time for her to move out.

She took the newspaper she'd picked up earlier into her room and slammed the door with a satisfying sound. After finding the Apartments for Rent section, she folded the paper and sat on the bed, propped up on her pillows.

She wasn't certain what part of town she should focus on. A job probably came first. The two companies looking for writers were nowhere near each other. She might have to wait until she had a job offer before making the decision about where would be most convenient area for her to live. Sherri tossed the newspaper onto the bed and rested her head against her knees.

* * *

"Sherri? Are you here?"

Greg closed the door behind him late that afternoon and looked around the apartment.

His place had never looked so good. The wood furniture gleamed with polish, the carpet had never been treated so well and there were no dirty dishes to be seen.

He appreciated the way Sherri had taken charge of the place, even washing his clothes. He had all the benefits of being married, except for one thing. That one thing was keeping him awake at night and causing him to take more cold showers than he'd ever had before.

The light scent of her perfume was everywhere. When he walked past the bathroom off the hallway, he could smell the shampoo she used. Each scent acted as an aphrodisiac on his system.

In other words, he needed in the worst way to make love to her, to drown himself in her scents and to keep her in bed for at least a week. He had a hunch that even a week wouldn't be enough.

Sharing the same apartment should have shown him her less attractive side. It was unfortunate that she didn't appear to have one. He would have expected anyone dealing with a break-in and losing everything she owned to show signs of stress and strain. Where was the short temper? The unreasonableness? The frustration about getting the matter settled?

Instead, she'd calmly and meticulously studied for exams without complaining or feeling sorry for herself.

How could he have fallen so hard so fast? If she had any idea of some of his more erotic thoughts about her, she'd be running down the street screaming for help.

"I'm here," she replied through the closed door to her room.

"I got some news about your case today."

She opened the door. "Really?"

She wore her school uniform of formfitting jeans and a top that was made out of some kind of material that clung to her, emphasizing her breasts and slender waist. He leaned against the hallway wall and felt himself going down for the third time.

"What is it?"

He turned away and headed for the kitchen. He got a soda out of the refrigerator. "Want one?" he asked over his shoulder.

"No, thanks."

She had followed him into the living room and now sat at the kitchen bar looking at him. "Tell me."

Greg stayed in the kitchen, resting against the back counter as far from her as possible. He drank some of the soda and tried to concentrate on the news he'd gotten earlier in the day.

"When forensics went over your apartment one of the men found a small shard of glass with blood on it. Otherwise, the place was clean. Whoever was there had obviously worn gloves. The glass must have slit the glove and nicked a finger. He may not have noticed in all the mayhem being created.

"Anyway, today we got a DNA match on the blood. We lucked out that he's already in the system."

Sherri looked relieved. "No kidding? Who is it?"

"A man who lives in Amarillo. That's why we didn't have a photo of the guy. We're going to need more evidence to arrest him but we're on the right track."

"What kind of motive would he have?"

"Our nice, charming family man who was murdered was shipping illegal drugs north. It's my guess he got crossways with his counterpart in Amarillo. He could have either stiffed him on the amount or the quality coming up from Mexico."

"That's horrible. His poor family."

"I know. The wife appeared to be stunned by that particular bit of news. After checking out her story we think she had no clue. His wife knew he was a successful businessman. What she didn't know was what his real business was."

"Why would some man in Amarillo worry about the possibility that I may have seen him?"

"Good question. But we know he was in your apartment. And we've been able to trace him to his boss in Amarillo, and he's the one we hope to get as well as the men who stabbed their Austin connection."

"What a relief," she said. Her look of gratitude flowed over him. *Remember, the look is only gratitude, nothing else.*

He nodded. "The local police in Amarillo told us that he has ties to individuals that the DEA is watching, so we're going to cooperate with the Amarillo police and the feds to build a strong case against all of them."

"I can't thank you enough for all you've done on this case."

"I can't take credit on this one. Most of the work was done in the lab. However, since we have two things to celebrate tonight I've made reservations at Henri's in town for us at seven. Is that okay with you?"

He was absolutely, positively irresistible when he grinned like that. She wanted to throw herself into his arms, hug and kiss him. Instead, she smiled and said, "Of course."

In anticipation of going out tonight she'd bought herself a new dress. She needed something to bolster her self-confidence when she told him she would be moving out. The red dress had tiny straps across the shoulders and hugged her body until it flared at her hips, ending above her knees.

He'd never seen her dressed up before and she definitely wanted to make an impression.

Greg finished his soda and said, "I'll see you later," and headed toward his bedroom, whistling.

At six-thirty Sherri heard his bedroom door open and his footsteps pass by her room. Without a mirror in the room, Sherri could only hope she looked all right.

Greg was thumbing through his mail and had opened a bill when he heard Sherri in the hallway. He glanced around and said, "It looks like—" His mouth dried up as soon as he saw her and every thought in his head left. He quickly checked that his jaw wasn't hanging open.

She looked up at him as she joined him in the living room. "It looks like what?"

"Uh. I don't remember. Wow, Sherri. You look great. I've never seen you in red before." What a stupid thing to say, but it was the most polite thing he could say as he took in her beauty. The dress showed off her shoulders and trim figure and she wore red strappy sandals that showed off her beautiful legs.

He glanced away and said, "If you're ready, we can go." His voice sounded hoarse. He now knew that he was a goner.

He'd booked a table at Henri's. Sherri looked around the room in awe. She had never been here before. A candle at each table created a series of oases in the otherwise shadowy room.

She and Greg followed the maître d' down the steps and to a table draped with a linen tablecloth. The maître d' pulled out one of the chairs and she slipped into it. Once Greg was seated they were handed menus.

A single rosebud in a vase sat next to the pillar candle.

The candle flame was reflected in Greg's eyes when he looked up from the menu. "Does anything look good to you?"

She avoided stating the obvious and forced herself to

look back at the menu that had no prices listed. "Hmm, well. I'm glad they put each item in English, even though it's in small print." How was she going to be able to order when she had no idea what anything cost?

"What would you like to have?" Greg asked.

She hesitated a moment and then said, "Why don't you order for both of us."

When the waiter appeared and introduced himself while filling their crystal glasses with water, Greg began speaking in what appeared to be fluent French. The waiter responded in the same language while Sherri looked on in amazement. The two men discussed the menu items; the waiter made notes on his pad and then left.

Greg smiled at her. "I hope you like seafood."

She nodded, hoping she didn't look as astonished as she felt. "You have all kinds of hidden talents, don't you?"

He looked at her and his ears turned red. He was embarrassed! How strange.

"Sorry. Guess I forgot myself there."

"You speak it like a native."

He nodded slowly. "I spent some time in France when I was younger."

"You keep surprising me, Greg. You talk so little about yourself."

"Because my life is fairly boring."

"Did you always want to work in law enforcement?"

"I played around with other options but I discovered I preferred detective work."

"Where were you born?"

"Connecticut."

"Really? Do you have any brothers or sisters?"

"A brother—Kyle."

"Do you see him often?"

"Um, no, I'm afraid not."

He looked relieved when their salads arrived and took the opportunity to change the subject.

Over dinner, Sherri said, "I feel like a princess. I've never been on a date like this before."

"I'm glad you're enjoying it. As a matter of fact, you look like a princess. All that's lacking is your tiara."

"Oh, darn. I knew I'd forget something!"

They shared a chuckle and continued with their meal.

By the time dessert and coffee arrived, Sherri knew that she'd never forget this night.

She decided to wait until tomorrow to tell Greg she would be moving out as soon as she found a job. She didn't want to be practical and prosaic and spoil the light mood and harmony they were sharing tonight.

"I propose a toast," Greg said, lifting his glass of wine. She picked up her glass and he said, "Congratulations for getting through finals without a nervous breakdown. I'm sure you aced everything."

They touched glasses and sipped on the wine.

"As long as we're making toasts," Sherri said, "thank you for helping me to deal with everything that's happened these past few weeks. Because I felt safe staying with you, I was able to focus and concentrate on finals."

They touched glasses once again.

"So," Greg said after a moment. "What next?"

She filled her lungs with air and slowly exhaled. "I'll be looking for a job and once I know where I'll be working, I'll find an apartment as near to work as possible."

"I've enjoyed having you with me."

She laughed nervously. "Oh, I bet. Having someone staying with you that you needed to babysit every night must have destroyed your love life these past few weeks."

He shook his head. "Not true. Mostly because I don't have time for a love life with the hours I work. How about you? Any boyfriends upset?"

"My group of friends understands why I've been staying with you and none of them are in the least jealous."

"If I was dating you, I'd be jealous as hell if you were living with another man."

His comment startled her. "You would?" Oh, my. He shouldn't have said that. Her body responded immediately and she could feel the heat in her face.

He reached over and took her hand, turning it over and tracing the lines on her palm. She had never thought of her palm as an erotic place until now, when steam must be coming out her ears.

"I know this sounds crazy to you, but I don't want to lose touch with you once you move away."

"Okay."

"The thing is, I've always been more comfortable on my own with no distractions. Until now. Now I want you in my life as much as you'll allow."

She closed her eyes, thinking she must be dreaming. When she opened them, she saw the heat in his and knew that he wanted her as badly as she wanted him.

"I'd like that."

He brought her palm up to his lips and kissed her. Sherri couldn't hide her shiver at the touch. "Do you still want to go to a movie tonight?" His voice sounded rough.

She could only shake her head.

"Me, either," he said with a wry smile. "What I want is to make love to you until we're both exhausted."

She took in a deep breath. Her fantasy and her dreams would be fulfilled if she only had the courage to agree. She turned her hand and slipped her fingers between his. "Let's go home."

Eleven

Neither spoke on the way home. Greg couldn't remember a time in his life when he'd been this nervous. But then, he'd never felt this way before. He was now operating in unfamiliar territory and hoped he didn't embarrass himself and offend Sherri.

Once home Greg helped her out of his car and offered her his hand, then the two of them climbed the steps to his apartment in silence.

He opened the door and, once they were inside, he closed and locked it.

He turned and saw that Sherri had moved over to the kitchen bar and put down her purse. Greg swallowed around the lump in his throat. She was so beautiful and he wanted her so much.

Sherri watched him warily. Who was supposed to make the first move? She'd imagined that as soon as they were alone they'd fall into each other's arms and let nature take over from there.

She'd obviously been reading too many romance novels. In those books passion overcame everything. Women didn't stand like ninnies and look at the men they were crazy about, waiting for some kind of a signal. She'd never been this intimate with anyone and she had no idea what came next.

He started toward her, which released her from her temporary paralysis. She met him halfway, and when he held his arms out she walked into the haven he offered. Greg leaned down while she went up on tiptoes and they finally kissed.

Yes! This was what she'd wanted since the one and only time he'd kissed her outside the police station. When he lifted her, she clung to him, her arms around his neck.

Greg wasted no time making his intentions clear. He ended the kiss and nibbled at her ear and neck before sliding his mouth back to hers. He vibrated with need and she clung to him, lost in the moment.

When he finally raised his head, Sherri discovered they were in his bedroom. She panicked. Of course she wanted Greg to make love to her. It was just that—

She closed her eyes. This was going so fast and she needed to— "Greg?"

He kissed her again. "Hmm?"

"I need to go to my room."

His head snapped back and he stared at her. "Now?" he said in disbelief.

"Uh-huh."

"Oh." He set her back on her feet and backed away from her as though he'd been burned. "Sorry. I didn't mean to—"

When he didn't say any more, she said, "It's okay," and almost ran to her room. The intensity of his lovemaking had overwhelmed her and she was on the verge of hyperventilating. How crazy was that?

I have to calm down. This is what I want. This is what I've wanted since moving in with him. She leaned her forehead on the door and took long, slow breaths.

When she could breathe normally Sherri undressed and waited until she heard Greg's door close before she went across the hallway to take a shower.

And think. Okay, so she'd overreacted. He must think she was a complete idiot.

She finally turned off the water and stepped out of the shower. After drying herself she wrapped the towel around herself and returned to her room. He was probably already asleep by now while she dithered about making love with him. Sherri looked in one of her drawers and pulled out a sleep shirt. Not a negligee, not even something slinky and sexy, because she didn't have anything coming close to that, but a sleep shirt—with kittens and puppies on it.

She pulled it over her head and carefully opened her bedroom door. She couldn't hear a thing.

He'd gone to sleep. She closed her eyes. She could not allow the evening to end on this note. If necessary she would go in there and wake him up. She'd tell him…something. Maybe confess her inexperience. She would also make it very clear that she wanted him very much.

Sherri walked silently down the hall to his door and was relieved to hear the faint sounds of the television. She closed her eyes and took several more deep breaths. She opened the door and stepped inside.

The only light in his room came from the television. He stared at her as though she were an apparition while she closed the door behind her.

She leaned against the door and looked at him. She was shaking and she was glad to have something to lean on.

"Either I'm dreaming or Sherri Masterson is now in my bedroom," he said, sounding wary.

"See what a great detective you are?" She attempted to sound sophisticated, as though she'd done this many times before. Her voice shook and didn't sound at all sophisticated.

He'd been propped up on pillows with the sheet at his waist and when she spoke he sat up. "I don't mean to sound crude or anything, but why, exactly, are you here?" He seemed to be having trouble with his breath.

She walked to the bed and sat beside him, so that their hips were touching. "I want to make love with you."

An eyebrow arched. "Are you sure? I got the feeling that you had changed your mind."

She shook her head. "It's just that…um…that I've never done this before and I'm a little out of my depth. So maybe, if you don't mind, you could teach me what—"

He interrupted her by grabbing her and falling sideways on the bed with her by his side. He turned to face her, his head resting on his fist. "You mean that you have never—"

"I know. It's ridiculous at my age."

"No, it's not," he said in a gentle voice, brushing a tendril of hair off her cheek. "You've been waiting and I don't want to do anything that would cause you to change your mind. We don't have to do this." He narrowed his eyes. "I mean that. I apologize for putting pressure on you."

"It's not that. Really. It's just that, if we could take it a little slower?"

He closed his eyes for a moment. "Are you really certain of that, Sherri?" he asked when he looked at her again.

She placed her hand on his chest and tentatively moved her fingers across his it. "I've wanted to touch you like this for what seems like forever."

"Be my guest," he said, his voice shaking.

She sat up and pushed him back on his pillow. Like a child with a new doll—a doll with an erection—she ran her fingers through his hair and trailed them down the side of his face and neck.

She leaned over and kissed one of his flat nipples and his body jerked but he didn't say anything. However, he was breathing harder. This time, she stroked his chest and continued downward, pushing the sheet away, revealing his engorged condition and that he slept in the nude. Her eyes widened.

She touched the drop of moisture with her finger and he grabbed her hand and pushed her backward. "Honey, you start that kind of exploring and I'm going to lose it, I guarantee you."

"Lose what?"

"Control. Do you have any idea how many walks I've taken at night trying to become tired enough to sleep while knowing you were just down the hall?"

She smiled. "I'm glad. Dreams about you have disturbed my sleep, too."

"Let me do the exploring," he said quietly. "There's just one thing that would help about now."

Sherri had trouble catching her breath. "What would that be?"

"If you'd remove your sleepwear. Take my word for it…you're not going to be sleeping much tonight, anyway."

She sat up and with jerky movements pulled the sleep shirt over her head, feeling awkward and exposed…until she saw his face. She allowed herself to relax and smiled at him.

Greg looked like a child on Christmas morning as he touched one of her breasts and watched the nipple draw into a tight bead. He leaned over and gently tugged on her breast with his mouth.

She could no longer lie still. When she shifted, he lifted

his head, cupped her cheek and kissed her with so much gentleness she thought she would melt.

He touched her tongue with his, thrusting and teasing before he pulled away from her. He cleared his throat. "Hold on. I'll be right back," he said and got up, striding to the bathroom. He was unconscious of his nude body—his beautifully proportioned body.

She heard him pull out a drawer and after a couple of seconds close it again. He appeared in the doorway—at full mast!—with a handful of condoms clutched in his hand.

He tossed them on the bedside table and was immediately back in his place. "Now, where were we?"

His teasing made her laugh. "I believe you were studying my body by Braille."

After that, her brain shut off. All she could do was feel and respond to his touch. He lightly pulled the tip of one breast into his mouth while caressing the other one. Eventually, he made a trail of kisses down her body, pausing to tongue her navel.

When he reached the juncture of her thighs, she stiffened and he sat up enough to move between her legs, where he knelt and looked at her.

"I don't want to hurt you," he whispered, running his hand across her curls and watching her response as his hand and fingers explored. She cried out and he increased the movement until she suddenly climaxed, calling out his name.

She couldn't believe the sensations flooding over her in waves.

Greg quickly put on protection and slowly leaned into her. She felt him touch her, slowly opening her to his entry. He moved forward and she opened up to him, loving the feel of his body on hers. Still caught up in new sensations, she lifted her hips to him, silently begging for more.

He took his time until he was completely sheathed inside her. "Am I hurting you?"

She shook her head, unable to speak at the moment. All she could do was to feel.

He continued to move, slowly at first until he let go of his strong self-control and let his needs take over. She climaxed with him this time. He dropped to his elbows, his forehead leaning against hers, breathing hard. He shifted slightly and rolled onto his side, gathering her in his arms.

Neither of them spoke for the longest time and Greg reluctantly moved away from her and went into the bathroom. She was too limp to move. She lay in the same place when he returned to bed.

He stretched out beside her and slid his arm under her head. She turned into him and placed her leg across his, settling her head on his shoulder. They lay quietly while the television made sounds in the background.

"Sherri?" Greg said after several minutes had gone by.

"Hmm?"

"I need to know something."

"Okay."

"Why did you make love with me tonight after waiting so long?"

"I've never met anyone I wanted to be with in this way until now."

"You continue to bring me to my knees. I've never wanted anyone the way I want you. I've never been so affected by a woman. You make me dizzy with desire, but that isn't all of it. You bring out feelings in me I never knew existed."

She turned her head and kissed him on the chest. "I'm glad. I feel the same way about you."

"I haven't been able to find a label to describe what I'm

feeling but I think all of that means I'm in love with you. Desperately in love with you. Can't-think-of-anything-else in love with you."

She raised her head and kissed him. When she finally pulled away, she murmured, "I feel the same way."

Without a word, he began making love to her again until they were both exhausted. They fell asleep in a tangle of arms and legs.

The next morning Sherri woke up alone in Greg's bed. She stretched and looked around. It was then she heard his shower going and she decided to join him.

She tapped on the open door and walked over to the shower stall. He stood with his head down, letting the water sluice over his head. He hadn't heard her. She opened the door and stepped inside with him.

They stayed in the shower until the water turned cold, dried off and went back to bed.

The next time she woke up she smelled coffee and opened her eyes. Greg stood beside the bed, watching her with gentle eyes and a slight smile on his face, holding two mugs of coffee.

She blinked and sat up to take the coffee. "You're dressed."

"Yep."

How silly was that, to state the obvious?

"Going to work?"

"Not today." He sat on the side of the bed and watched her. The coffee tasted as good as it smelled and she breathed in the aroma as she sipped. She didn't say any more because he didn't seem to want to talk.

She'd fallen in love with the tall, dark and silent type of male. He didn't make idle conversation. She could grow used to a hunk like that.

When she finished, he took her cup and set both of them on the table by the bed.

"I guess you know how I feel about you after last night."

"You also know how I feel about you," she replied and they both smiled.

"Here's the thing," he went on after a moment. "Given our feelings for each other, I'd like to get married. How do you feel about that?"

He was nervous. Didn't he know the answer to that?

"I'd very much like to marry you," she said softly.

He pulled her into his lap and hugged her.

"I need to put some clothes on," she said. "You have me at a disadvantage here," she added, kissing his chin. "We haven't known each other very long and I think we should wait a little while, don't you?" He let her get up. She wrapped the top sheet that hung half off the bed around her. "When did you have in mind? Late fall, early spring?"

"How about today?"

"Yeah, sure. I'm serious. We need to take time to get to know each other better. We've known each other for about two weeks. That doesn't give us time to—"

"Sherri, I'll get on my knees if I have to but I want us to get married as soon as possible. We know each other in all the ways that count. Regardless of the length of time, we've lived together, learned each other's habits. There's no reason to wait."

"Today?" she repeated slowly.

"Uh-huh."

"This is crazy, you know that."

"Don't I know it! I never intended to get married at all and here I am pleading with you."

His sheer physical presence was bad enough, but when

he spoke like that, there was no way she could resist him. "All right."

"Good. Get dressed and we'll go get our license. At least we salvaged your birth certificate from your wrecked apartment."

"What about your family? I don't have any, but didn't you once say—"

"I'll call Millie. I bet she'll let us have the service at her home. It's time you met her."

So Millie was his only family. How sad that they should both be without parents. Now they would have to form a family for themselves.

This marriage would work out. She would labor hard to make it do so.

Twelve

Sherri opened her eyes, feeling disoriented. She'd been dreaming about a time when she'd been married. She had gone into her marriage without a clue as to how to be a wife or what was expected of her. She'd tried to model the relationship on the one her parents had had, but it had been no use. Her dad had worked nine to five with two weeks off for vacation, a homebody comfortable hanging out with his family. Greg's personality couldn't be more different.

She looked around Millie's bedroom. She had loved that woman. She and Greg had spent any free time they happened to have with her. When Millie met Sherri for the first time and Greg told her they wanted to get married right away, Millie had asked her pastor if he would come to her home to perform the wedding service.

Sherri had thought about asking some of her friends to attend, but they had scattered after finals and wouldn't be back until graduation. She'd asked Greg if he wanted to invite friends or coworkers and he'd shaken his head no. "You're the only one that's important to me. If you're there, I'm happy."

The next several months had been fun. Sherri had felt as though she were playing house. She'd been hired at the place that had just let her go last week, and she'd made enough money that they didn't have to worry that she would bankrupt Greg.

They had kept separate bank accounts and shared expenses. Greg treated her like a princess. On their second anniversary he had actually bought her a tiara.

It was soon after that anniversary that everything seemed to fall apart.

She'd certainly grown up through the experience. She'd believed everything he'd said and implied…until she had discovered he had a life he'd never told her about. When she'd tried to talk to him about what she'd found out, he'd turned around and walked out of the room…or the apartment.

He hadn't trusted her enough to talk about his past, to let her in and help her understand him better. Knowing that was the beginning of the end. She'd distanced herself for protection and had been devastated by his lack of trust.

At the end she'd known she would have to get away from him, despite the fact she was still in love with him. He'd become someone she didn't know and she could no longer live with him. It had been too painful.

Now, here she was, living in Millie's home with Greg. What was she going to do? She needed to get well as soon as possible in order to get away from him.

It couldn't happen soon enough.

She got out of bed and hopped into the bathroom, hanging

on to whatever furniture was on the way. Her incision protested, so once she'd finished in the bathroom she took her time getting back to her chair.

She gathered her clothes from drawers and the closet and awkwardly got dressed. Once she got her arm out of its cast, she would be able to use crutches until her leg healed.

The doctor had mentioned putting on a walking cast in a few weeks. She'd be able to apply for jobs. She didn't dare rent anything until she knew what her salary would be.

Her situation mirrored what she'd gone through when she'd first met Greg. But she'd never dreamed that two years after her divorce she would find herself depending on him once again.

Yet here she was, in his debt with nowhere else to turn. She would have to be strong enough to see him every day without getting involved with him again.

Piece of cake, right? She knew better than that.

She steeled herself and went in search of coffee.

When she reached the large kitchen, Sherri saw Hannah preparing something that smelled delicious.

"Good morning," Sherri said, feeling awkward.

Hannah turned and saw her. "Why, good morning! You should have buzzed me and I would have helped you dress."

"I need to learn to take care of myself."

Hannah nodded. "I understand. Just don't forget to call me when you need a little assistance."

"What is that wonderful smell?"

"I'm making cinnamon rolls. Would you like some?"

"Yes, thank you."

"Coffee, orange juice and water are set on the table in the other room. I'll be right there."

Sherri paused in the doorway to the smaller dining room. Greg sat at the table where they had eaten the night before, his back to her, reading the paper and sipping coffee. She needed no reminders of his habits. After being married to him, she knew a great deal about his daily routine, his likes and dislikes, his hobbies and his favorite teams. She'd been so naive back then, thinking that it didn't matter that he didn't talk about the past. She'd presumed that whatever had happened had been traumatic and he didn't want to be reminded of it. She'd felt certain that their love for each other would be enough on which to build a strong marriage, but whatever they had when they married had been chased away by the tension between them.

Sherri moved toward the table on silent wheels. Greg glanced around and saw her. She'd never figured out how he could do that.

"Morning. Did you sleep okay?" he asked politely.

"I slept fine, thank you," she replied, equally polite.

It wasn't long until Hannah arrived with two plates, sliding them in front of each of them. Sherri had already drunk half of her coffee. "Thank you, Hannah."

Greg laid the paper aside. "Thanks, Hannah. I was going into withdrawal without these."

Hannah laughed and went back to the kitchen, leaving Greg and Sherri alone.

Sherri refilled her cup from the carafe on the table and then took a bite of the most heavenly cinnamon bun she'd ever tasted. "No wonder you go into withdrawal without these. They're delicious."

He smiled. After a moment he said, "I'm surprised to see you up this early. You were never a morning person."

"I don't know what time it is. I guess I must have slept all I wanted to."

"Are you feeling better this morning?"

"Much. I'm glad to be out of the hospital."

Greg glanced at his watch and stood. "If you need anything today, give me a call and I'll pick it up on my way home."

There were so many things she wanted to say. She thought it wiser to answer with a nod. She wanted to keep their present relationship polite, cordial.

She watched him leave the house and stride across the lawn to the garage. He disappeared around the tall hedge. A few minutes later she heard his car drive away.

They had gotten through another time together. Now she could relax until he showed back up sometime this evening.

Greg pulled up at the station and parked. Once inside, he relaxed a little. He was in his element here: doing his job, solving cases, testifying in court. These were things he understood.

Once Greg arrived at his desk, Pete came over and claimed the chair beside it. "How did yesterday go?"

"Mornin', Sarge," Greg drawled. "It's good to see you, too."

"Yeah, yeah. What did she say when you took her to your home?"

"About what you'd expect. She considers me to be high-handed and overbearing."

"Well, of course, that's to be expected, since you are. But besides that?"

"Nothing's changed between us, if that's what you want to know. She tolerates me, but that's all."

"Sorry to hear that. You guys were so happy for the first couple of years. I was sort of hoping that once you spent more time with each other again, you'd be able to work things out between you."

"All you need is a diaper and a bow and arrow, Cupid. But do me a favor—point that arrow at someone else, okay?"

Pete got up from his chair and shrugged. "All I know is that you've been miserable since the day she walked out. Maybe the two of you can at least bridge the chasm between you, even if you go your own ways afterward." He studied Greg for a couple of minutes, which made Greg nervous. He picked up a file and began to look through it.

"You know, Greg, you could have bought her a place and hired someone to look after her. You didn't have to take her home with you."

Greg didn't look up from the file in front of him. "Now why didn't I think of that?"

"I think you want her back and now's your chance while she can't get up and walk away. Of course, you're too stubborn to admit your motives."

Greg laughed. "You just keep thinking that, Cupid, while I get to work."

"You're a good man, Hogan," Pete said, turning away.

"Yeah? How about telling the captain that? He's on my case again."

"Nothing new about that."

Greg sighed and leaned back in his chair. "He can find the darnedest things to gripe about."

"He's afraid you're after his job."

Greg rolled his eyes. "Why would I want an administrative job? I enjoy working in the field."

"Buy him a Hallmark card to let him know he has your vote for remaining in his position."

Greg's answer was terse and unprintable.

Pete laughed and walked away.

Greg smiled to himself. Hadn't he been thinking earlier about being comfortable on the job? Well, putting up with the captain was part of it.

Pete was wrong. He hadn't been miserable with Sherri out of his life. A little bored, perhaps. She had added a sparkle to his life. But that was then. Now she wanted to be as far away from him as possible. She'd certainly made that clear. Yeah, he'd harbored some hopes that they could sit down and calmly talk about what had happened. The problem was that Sherri spoke in code. He didn't have a clue what he'd done that was so bad she'd chosen to end the marriage.

He would probably never know.

Maybe Pete was right. He might find a place for her to live. Tell her it's a rental, set the amount to something she could afford. He knew without a doubt that she would refuse to accept the place if she knew he'd bought it for her.

The thing he needed to watch out for was getting attached to her again. As long as she was as cool and distant toward him as she'd been during breakfast, he wouldn't have to make much of an effort.

Greg forced himself to focus on his job. No sense in giving the captain something else to gripe about.

Thirteen

Greg arrived home two weeks later to the sound of laughter and splashing from the pool area. When he stepped through the gate he saw Sven, Hannah, Sherri and a well-built man he didn't know gathered around the pool. Who was the guy? Not that it mattered to him. She could have a half-dozen men hanging around if it made her happy.

Hannah saw him and waved. "Come join us, Greg. We're celebrating."

He walked over to the pool. Sven and Hannah must have been in it recently because their suits were wet. Not a bad idea. The day had been a scorcher.

"Celebrating what?"

The man stood and walked over to him, holding out his hand. "Hi. I'm Troy. I'll be working with Sherri for a few sessions to help her strengthen the muscles in her arm and leg."

Behind him, Sherri held up her broken arm and he saw that

it was no longer in a cast. "I also got a walking cast on my leg. The doctor said I'm healing nicely."

She sat in one of the lounge chairs beside the pool, wearing—almost wearing—a bikini. Her body was exposed to everyone around and he hated the idea of other men seeing her like that.

He turned and walked into the house. He went to the refrigerator and got a beer. After taking a long swallow, he rubbed the cold bottle across his forehead.

Why not join them? After the week he'd had, he deserved to relax a little. With that thought in mind Greg went upstairs, changed into his bathing suit and grabbed a towel. He draped the towel around his neck and went back outside.

He walked to the small diving board at the deep end, bounced a couple of times and dived into the pool. The water caressed him like liquid silk. He swam the length of the pool underwater and came up near Sven and Hannah.

"Wow." He heard Troy's voice. Greg turned his head and Troy continued, "You're in great shape."

For an old guy, Greg finished what he hadn't said. "I swim a lot, mostly at night when I can't sleep." Which had been almost every night since Sherri came.

He glanced over at Sherri and was startled to see her staring at him with a heated gaze. He recognized her expression because he'd seen it often the first couple of years they were married.

The look had always turned him on, and today was no different.

He turned and swam back to the other end of the pool. The size of the pool was a blessing. As long as he stayed away from her she wouldn't be able to see how much she turned him on.

Now that she was more mobile it was time for him to look for a place for her to live, somewhere in another part of town so that he wouldn't be running into her at the local shops and post office.

He swam back and forth while Sven, Hannah and Troy stayed at the four-foot end. Eventually Hannah and Sven left. A little later Troy took his leave, leaving Sherri in the chair and making a date to come back in a few days.

And then there were two. Greg stopped in the middle of the pool and looked at her. She smiled.

"Do you realize that's the first time you've smiled at me in years?"

"I'm happy."

He swam over to her. "For good reason. Your doctor must be impressed with your improvement and so am I." Greg stood waist high in water while Sherri watched him. "Are you ready to go inside?" he asked, his hands on his hips.

She sighed with contentment. "All right."

Sherri waited until Greg pulled himself out of the water and pushed his hair back from his face. Once he was beside her chair she offered him her hand. He pulled her up, using enough momentum that she toppled into his arms.

"You've been driving me crazy in that poor excuse for a swimsuit. You know that, don't you?"

He kissed her. Not an exploratory kiss, but one of passion and need. He braced himself, knowing she would be angry. Instead, she eagerly returned the kiss. He stood there and kissed and caressed her until he knew he had to stop. Otherwise he'd be hauling her pretty butt into the house to make love to her.

He forced himself to step back, steadying her by grasping her upper arms. She looked away from him, breathing as hard as he was. Damn. He hadn't needed a reminder of how good she felt in his arms.

Without a word, Sherri reached for a cane that he hadn't

noticed beside the chair. He grabbed his towel, patted himself dry and wrapped the towel around his waist.

She started along the path toward the house. She was handling the cane with ease. "Why am I driving you crazy?" she asked over her shoulder.

He walked along behind her. "I thought I could have you here and not be bothered by your presence. More fool, I."

"I didn't ask to be here," she said quietly.

"I know."

She took the stairs to the terrace one at a time with little hesitation. Once inside, they moved toward the front hallway.

Sherri stopped in front of her room and turned to face him. "Thank you."

"For what?"

"For treating me with such courtesy these past few weeks. I'm sorry that it's been a strain on you."

"I'll survive." He walked away from her and trotted up the stairs. She watched him until he was out of her sight.

She'd almost come out of her chair earlier when she got her first glimpse of Greg striding across the lawn in his swimsuit. The man was too darn good-looking for his own good and hot, hot, hot.

And that kiss. She closed her eyes. She'd tried to ignore him while he was swimming, but her eyes had kept straying back to him. She really didn't need the reminder of what he could do to her with just a look. And a kiss? Mmm-mmm. She'd have to stay away from him for the rest of the day.

That evening they had dinner out on the terrace. Greg almost groaned out loud when he saw the table set for two. Was Hannah trying to play matchmaker? That's all he needed. He was already feeling vulnerable. How could he have been so stupid as to kiss her, no matter the provocation? All he'd been thinking about was the heated look in her eyes. Once he'd touched her, her response had made him forget everything but his need for her.

He went into the kitchen and got a beer. Hannah was placing the food on plates and it smelled delicious. He'd been too busy to eat lunch today and now his stomach growled in protest.

Hannah laughed. "I'm glad to know you're hungry this evening."

He looked at what she had made. "This is kind of a fancy dinner, isn't it?"

She glanced up. "Well, I thought it should be special for the celebration."

"What cele—" He felt like a fool. "Of course. Sherri is coming along nicely."

Sherri saw them in the kitchen and paused in the doorway. "I must have put on twenty pounds since I got here, Hannah. I'm going to have to go on a diet, but it will have been worth it. Everything looks and smells delicious."

Greg looked at Sherri but she wouldn't meet his eyes. "Wine?" he asked, holding up a bottle of her favorite.

She glanced at him nervously before looking away. "Yes, thank you."

Greg helped Hannah carry everything outside while Sherri trailed behind. "Oh! How lovely. You've really outdone yourself this evening, Hannah."

Hannah watched them as they sat and checked to see they had everything they needed before she said, "Thank you. Enjoy your meal."

After a couple of glasses of wine Sherri managed to relax. The food was out of this world and what could be better than the view of the back lawn, the pool and the blooming bushes and flowerbeds?

The two of them didn't have much to say during dinner and, after Hannah cleared everything away except for the wine bottle and glasses, she told them good-night.

Sherri sighed. "What a beautiful night. Look. The moon is just now appearing. Must be a full moon."

Greg didn't look at her or the rising moon. Instead, he finished the wine in his glass and poured another one.

"I have a question for you," Greg said into the quiet several minutes later.

Sherri turned her head and looked at him. "Is your question going to ruin the peace and quiet of this beautiful night?"

He didn't answer, which was an answer in itself.

Oh well, the wine had mellowed her enough, she hoped, to hear the question without getting upset.

"Shoot."

"That wouldn't be my choice of words," he replied.

"I'll rephrase, counselor. What is your question?"

"You're not going to like it."

"Yes, I've already gotten that."

"I was thinking about the day I came home and discovered that you had moved out of our apartment…without a warning, without an explanation, without a phone call. I've racked my brain in an effort to think about what had happened the day before, or even the week before, to cause you to walk out like that."

She held out her empty glass. "I need more, please," she said politely. He poured the rest of the wine into her glass without saying anything. She took it and sipped. Finally, she said, "Do you remember the evening when I first asked you why you never mentioned your parents?"

He didn't answer right away. "Not really."

"I didn't think it made much of an impression on you,

even though I tried to talk to you about them another time or two after that."

His face was in shadows. "You left me because I wouldn't talk about my parents?" he asked in disbelief.

"No."

"That's good to know."

"It was all of the things you never told me. You led me to believe your only relatives were Millie and a brother."

"I never said that."

"Correct. You never said anything. I was visiting Millie one afternoon and I asked her when your parents had died. That's when I discovered all kinds of things I didn't know before, such as that they were very much alive and lived in Connecticut. She mentioned that not only had you graduated from Harvard with a bachelor's degree, you had also graduated from Harvard Law School with top grades."

"And that's upsetting because…?"

"I realized that I really didn't know you at all. We'd been living together for over two years. I'd shared with you everything about my life, which I must admit wasn't as colorful as yours. You mentioned you'd been in France at one time. How about your lengthy stays in Italy and the U.K.? What upset me was that you didn't trust me enough to share any of that with me."

"It wasn't a matter of trust," he said tersely. "It was…" His voice faded away.

"Your past makes up who you are…your experiences, your traumas, your triumphs all contribute to the man you are today. Yet you chose not to share any of it with me. You were treating me like a live-in girlfriend who kept your bed warm at night, but who wasn't important enough to open up and talk to."

"You were very important to me. I loved you. I thought I made that clear."

"As long as we were only playing house together and I didn't make any waves. Do you remember the day I pointed out that we'd never talked about having children, and you said you'd make a terrible father?"

"Believe me, I would."

"Okay. But why had you never mentioned to me before that you didn't want children?"

"I guess because I never thought it was important."

"There were too many things that we didn't discuss before we got married that we should have."

"I don't get it. You left me because I didn't talk to you and tell you how I felt about everything?"

"About *any*thing. The child issue was of real concern to me at the time because I thought I was pregnant."

Greg had been leaning back in his chair when she spoke and sat up abruptly. "You were pregnant?"

"I don't know. I missed a period. I wasn't just late. I missed it."

"Why in hell didn't you tell me!"

"The thing was, bringing up our views of a family was my naive way of broaching the subject. Since we'd never discussed it, I thought it was time."

"You should have told me anyway."

"By then we rarely spoke, unless it was about what to have for dinner or who was going to drop off the clothes at the cleaners. Sometimes we managed to converse about whatever was in the mail any particular day. I had already faced the fact that I didn't want to have a marriage like that, a marriage where certain subjects were not to be discussed. Even if I *had* been pregnant, I wouldn't have stayed, given your feelings about the subject."

Sherri discovered that she wasn't at all upset by discussing that time in her life. She'd worked through the pain; she'd dealt with the sense of betrayal. She'd even dealt with Greg's lack of trust. She felt as though she was talking about someone else who had suffered through that time in her life.

She finished her wine and yawned. "I'm going to turn in," she said to Greg as she stood.

"Sherri?"

She'd only taken a couple of steps when he spoke. She turned around. He stood, silhouetted by the strong moonlight. "I wish you'd told me back then," he said in a low voice.

"Would it have made any difference, or would you have brushed it all away as you had so many times before and told me that I was overreacting? Would we have ended up in bed together, as though lovemaking was the cure for everything that was going wrong in our relationship?"

"I never meant to hurt you."

"And I never meant to hurt *you*. My leaving was my way of surviving an untenable situation."

She turned around and walked inside. Looking back to that time in her life, she might have done things differently. She'd been so young and idealistic back then. She'd believed in all the love songs she'd ever heard. She'd believed in happily ever after. Eventually she came to understand that happily ever after could be living alone with her cat and not having to deal with continuing heartache.

Greg stayed outside. He walked over to the pool, stripped out of his clothes and dived in. He swam furiously as though all the sharks in the world were after him. When he finally stopped by the side of the pool he was gasping for breath.

The moon now rode high in the sky, casting its light.

He crawled out of the pool and, dripping water, gathered

his clothes and went inside. Once in his room, he tossed his clothes aside and went in to take a shower. With the heavy spray of water beating down on him, Greg finally allowed himself to think about what Sherri had said tonight.

There was very little emotion in the telling, that was the first thing he'd noticed. She'd loved him back then. He knew that. She did not love him now. It had been obvious in her voice and demeanor.

Like it or not, he knew that he didn't have a snowball's chance in hell of winning her back.

The next morning Greg went downstairs to find the coffee made but no sign of Hannah. That's when he remembered that she'd asked for the day off in order to help Sven at the nursery.

He'd spent a restless night going over everything that Sherri had told him last night. It wasn't that he hadn't trusted her. He had erased his parents from his life and saw no reason to discuss them. It hadn't been a lack of trust in her. No. He trusted her then and he trusted her now. But maybe he'd been a little high-handed with her.

She'd certainly been right about one thing: those last few months had been miserable. So maybe she'd done the right thing. She'd definitely done the right thing for her.

He knew what he needed to do. He'd go looking for a place to buy for Sherri. She didn't have to know he was the owner. He'd have a rental place take care of all that. He'd call a Realtor later in the morning to find out what was out there.

Without turning around, he knew that Sherri was nearby. He didn't really understand it, but he seemed to have an antenna that only worked where she was concerned. He turned around. "Coffee?"

She looked around the kitchen. "Yes, please. Is Hannah sick?"

"Uh, no. I'd forgotten until I came in here that yesterday morning Hannah asked for the day off. She's working with Sven today." He walked over to the refrigerator. "What would you like for breakfast?"

"I'll have toast. I can make it."

He poured two glasses of orange juice and carried them to the dining room table. When he returned to the kitchen, Sherri was buttering toast. Without saying anything, he picked up a tray and put the carafe, their two cups and her plate of toast on it.

"Do you want some?" she asked.

"Not now. It's nice to have the day off. I'll make something after a while."

They sat down and Sherri took a piece of toast and began to eat.

"Will Troy be here today?" he asked, breaking the silence.

"No. Monday. I have some exercises I can do." She looked out the window. "Looks like another nice day."

"Yes. I'd enjoy it more if it wasn't so blasted hot." So it had come down to talking about the weather. He supposed that was all they had left to discuss.

Sherri finished her toast and juice, then poured another cup of coffee. "I've made a couple of appointments this afternoon. I should have planned better. I think I've found a possible apartment. My problem is getting there."

"I can take you."

She smiled. "Thank you. I had planned to ask Hannah. She's run me to the store a few times. I should have checked with her first."

"No problem. I don't have anything else planned."

They looked at each other. He could see that she had no problem with moving out and she wasn't going to wait for him to buy a place. Probably just as well. She'd been right about something else. A clean break was the better way to leave their relationship.

Even so, there was no way he could have ignored the fact she'd been hospitalized because of a wreck. Everything he'd done after that was for her benefit, not his. At no time did Sherri give him reason to hope that she would come back to him. He'd been fantasizing. Now, he had to face reality.

"I've also managed to take a temporary job that I can do at home. That will bring in enough money to pay bills until I find a permanent one."

"You've been busy."

"I was waiting for the walking cast. There's really no need to take advantage of your hospitality any longer."

It was definitely time to cut his losses and get on with his life.

Greg heard the doorbell. He glanced at his watch. It was almost eleven. They'd both slept in this morning. Since Hannah was gone, he'd better see who it was.

The bell rang a second time before he reached the door. An impatient sort, whoever it was. He opened the door and his jaw dropped.

"If Mohammed won't come to the mountain, the mountain must come to Mohammed. Hello, darling."

Fourteen

Greg looked at the three people standing at the front door and cleared his throat. "What a surprise. Come in."

He stepped back and watched as his parents, Max and Katrina, together with Penelope, the woman his mother had wanted him to marry years ago, walked into his home.

His mother gave him an air kiss, his father lifted an eyebrow and Penelope threw herself into his arms. "Oh, Greg, I've missed you so much! It's great to see you after all this time!" She kissed him with exuberance. When he didn't respond she stepped back with an embarrassed laugh. "It's not fair that the years have merely added to your good looks."

He nodded to the living room. "Shall we?" he said to all of them in general. He escorted his unexpected and unwelcome company into the formal living room. "May I get you something to drink?" he asked politely.

Katrina said, "Iced tea, please."

Penelope nodded.

"Father?"

"Nothing for me." Max was making it clear that he had been coerced into coming by taking a seat as far away from all of them as possible. Greg and his father knew exactly where they stood with each other.

Instead of going directly to the kitchen—of all days for Hannah to be gone—he went back into the dining room. "Sherri?"

She looked at him in surprise. "There's somebody here for me?"

"You could look at it that way. As I recall from last night's discussion, you left me because I refused to discuss my parents with you. Well, here's your chance to find out all my deep, dark secrets."

She stood. "What are you talking about?"

"It seems that my parents have come for a visit. Now you'll be able to find out all about my 'other life' that you wanted to know."

Her jaw dropped. "Your parents? They're here?"

"Yes. I have absolutely no idea why they're here, but I'm sure I'm about to find out. I would like your help."

"Have they ever been here before?"

"No."

"What do you want me to do?"

"Be your usual gracious self."

"Now you're being sarcastic."

"No, I'm not. You've always been gracious. I need that today because it's next to impossible for me to be."

He walked with her into the hallway and said, "Hold on. I've got to get some refreshments."

She looked bewildered. "I really don't understand. How is my being here going to be a help to you?"

"I know I'm asking a lot from you, but will you please go along with whatever I say?" Greg spoke in a soft tone. "I will be eternally grateful if you will."

"Greg, I have never seen you this upset. What's going on?"

He clenched his jaw. "You'll find out soon enough." He went into the kitchen, filled two glasses with ice and tea and returned to her side.

Greg paused in the wide doorway of the living room. "Mother? Father? Penelope? This is Sherri Masterson. We were married five years ago." He didn't dare look at Sherri. The statement was a fact, after all. Instead, he handed Katrina and Penelope their drinks. They took them, both looking stunned.

Greg walked beside Sherri until they reached one of the sofas. He helped her sit and settled in beside her. "Sherri was in a bad wreck several weeks ago. We were both grateful she wasn't killed. It's a miracle she's alive today."

Katrina and Penelope were so much alike in their mannerisms as they looked Sherri over from head to toe with undisguised disapproval that they could have rehearsed the scene. He should be amused by their behavior, but he tended to lose his sense of humor where his family was concerned.

Sherri glanced at them and then at Greg. He casually put his arm on the back of the sofa behind her.

Katrina was the first to speak. "Did he say Masterson?"

Sherri nodded with a small smile on her face. The smile made him nervous. She knew she had him at her mercy. He could only hope she didn't decide that it was payback time. He sighed with relief with her short answer.

"Yes."

"What part of the country are you from?" his mother asked.

"I was born in Texas. I lived in a small ranching community in the Hill Country until I moved to Austin to attend university."

"Well," Katrina finally said. "I doubt that I know your family, then."

"No. My parents were killed in a plane crash several years ago."

Greg watched Katrina and Penelope exchange glances. This was so not amusing.

Katrina said, "You're looking fit, Greg." She paused, as though searching for words. "I suppose that marriage agrees with you."

He looked at Sherri and she grinned at him. She was actually *enjoying* his discomfort.

"Would it have hurt you to have told us about it? I'm surprised that Grandmother never told me."

"I understand that she rarely, if ever, heard from you."

Katrina's eyelids fluttered. "Well, I have such a busy schedule and Millie and I never had very much in common. I could never understand why you enjoyed visiting with her so much when you were a child."

He could tell her the truth, that Millie had been his escape from an oppressive household, but there was no reason to hurt his mother. She was who she was and was admired by many people. She'd just been a lousy mother.

"I liked her," he finally said. "She was fun to be around."

"Well," Katrina conceded, "she was always a little eccentric."

Greg laughed and looked at Sherri, who was trying *not* to laugh. "I'll have to agree with you on that."

Katrina looked at him with a puzzled expression. "I have never understood why you were so secretive."

Sherri's elbow connected with Greg's ribs and he coughed,

trying to cover the fact that he'd flinched. That had hurt. He took her hand and placed it on his knee and smiled at her.

"You know, that's an excellent question. I suppose it was because I wanted to keep Sherri all to myself." He leaned over and kissed her cheek.

Penelope cleared her throat and Greg glanced at her. "I'm sorry, Penelope. I didn't mean to leave you out of the conversation."

She did not look happy. "I probably shouldn't have come."

"Nonsense, dear," Katrina replied quickly, "I wanted you to come." She looked at Greg. "The reason we decided to come was to see if you would consider moving back east. Since Millie is gone, there's no reason for you to continue to stay here. I knew if I called to tell you we were coming that you'd put us off, which is why we decided to surprise you. Since Penelope had been asking about you quite a bit, I invited her to come along."

Penelope blushed an unflattering shade of red. Katrina looked at Sherri. "Penelope has been a close family friend since she and Greg were children. Her family owns the estate next to ours and the two of them often played together."

Katrina continued. "Penelope recently returned from living in Italy. She was married to a young man whose family can be traced back to the Middle Ages. Some kind of prince or count," she said airily, waving her hand in the air.

Penelope looked as though she'd swallowed something bitter.

Greg nodded and smiled at Penelope. She didn't return the gesture.

"So what's your married name, Penny?"

"Now, Greg," Katrina hastily said. "You know how she detests being called by that nickname, surely you haven't forgotten! Penelope took her maiden name back after the divorce."

Sherri squeezed his hand a little too forcefully. He brought it up and kissed her knuckles, giving her a loving smile and a narrowed gaze.

Greg glanced over at Max. "I'm surprised to see that you left your fiefdom. How in the world did Mother persuade you to come?"

Katrina trilled into laughter. "Don't be silly, Greg. Your father wanted to see you as much as I did!"

His mother was still living in her own fantasy world, it seemed.

"Do you have help to take care of this place?" she asked.

"Yes. She's working with her husband today. They have a nursery."

"Oh." Katrina looked at Sherri. "I suppose you have trouble being able to do much around the house."

"That's true," Sherri said blandly.

"Well." Katrina seemed to run out of things to say. She looked at Max, who sat with his head resting on the back of his chair and his eyes closed. "Max!" she said irritably. "I don't know why you don't sit over here and join in the conversation."

"I have nothing to say. As for my fiefdom, as you put it, Greg, I have a board of directors that somehow manages to keep me in line. Your brother is doing quite well in the company, by the way."

"Good for Kyle."

Katrina said, "Oh, Greg, you really must come back…at the very least for a visit. Kyle and Marsha have the smartest children. They're absolutely adorable." She paused and looked at Sherri. "I take it you don't have children, yet, do you? Marsha's the earth-mother type and enjoys rearing her brood."

Greg searched for something to say that wasn't impossibly rude, but before he could think of anything Sherri surprised him

by saying, "Oh, we don't have children, yet. I had just graduated from the university when we married," she said confid-
ingly, giving Penelope a quick glance. "We wanted a few years
together before we began our family. Although—" she paused
and gave Greg a melting glance "—we were just discussing
children last night, weren't we, honey? If I hadn't been
involved in that accident, I'd probably be pregnant right now."

Greg almost choked. Sherri looked at him and said, "I
know, sweetheart. I was disappointed, too."

Nobody said anything.

Not a thing.

The room resounded with silence.

Finally, Katrina said, "Well, I know you must have plans
for today and we don't want to keep you. We're staying at the
Omni while we're here and we'd like to take you out to dinner
this evening."

Once again, Sherri spoke before Greg could open his
mouth. "Why, that would be so nice, Mother Hogan. I hope
I can call you that." Katrina's face registered her distaste.
"Greg has told me so much about you and I would love to get
to know you better." She looked at Penelope and smiled
gently. "I'm sorry. I'm afraid he never mentioned his childhood friend. I'm looking forward to hearing all the stories you
must know about him when he was a child."

Max stood. "We'll see you tonight, then. Come to the hotel
at seven and we'll go from there."

"I'll see about reservations at one of the restaurants,"
Katrina added, also coming to her feet. Penelope looked as if
she couldn't wait to escape.

"Please excuse me for not getting up," Sherri said, smiling
at each of them.

Greg said, "I'm sure they understand, darling." He gave

her a brief squeeze and stood. He walked them to the door. "We'll see you tonight." His mother gave him another air kiss. This time, Penelope followed Katrina's example.

Once he opened the door, the three of them filed outside to the waiting BMW limousine. The driver hopped out of the front seat and went around the car, opening the doors for them.

Watching this activity, Greg thought, *I wonder if my father had the driver bring his limo down. Wouldn't put it past him.*

With a big sigh of relief he went back inside the house and headed to the living room. He and Sherri had a few things to discuss.

Fifteen

Sherri was coming toward him when he reached the doorway. She gave him a cheerful smile.

"Why did you accept that dinner invitation when you knew I didn't want to go?"

"Why did you never tell me that you came from money?"

They stared at each other. "It wasn't important."

"Essentially, nothing was important to you but getting me into bed."

"That's not fair! I—" He ran his hand through his already tousled hair. "To hell with it." He turned on his heel and headed upstairs. He heard Sherri's door close softly.

What an unholy mess. Sherri hadn't mentioned their divorce, but he almost wished she had. Or better yet, he shouldn't have had her meet them at all.

He hadn't been thinking straight. Sherry was no longer a part of his life, or wouldn't be in another week or two. He didn't owe his parents an explanation of his life. Just as he didn't owe Sherri an explanation—

He had shut her out in the same way he'd shut his parents out. He didn't like talking about himself or rehashing his past with anyone. Not just Sherri. Why couldn't she have understood that?

He'd fallen hard for her, had never felt anything like it before. He'd loved her to the best of his abilities and it hadn't been enough for her. He must be too much of a loner to have a relationship with anyone.

There was no help for it; he would be having dinner with his parents and Penny tonight. That one hadn't aged well. She was too thin and too tense. Of course, finding out he was married could have caused the last part. He smiled. It had been worth putting up with Sherri's crazy sense of humor not to have Penelope Prissy Pants, his childish name for her—which he'd wisely never said out loud—fawning over him all evening.

Greg and Sherri arrived at the hotel a few minutes before seven. Greg handed the car keys to the valet and helped Sherri out of the car.

She looked stunning tonight, wearing a dress he'd never seen before. Then again, there had been no reason for her to dress up before.

She'd chosen a green dress made of some kind of shimmery material that draped over her body in a very sensual way. Even using a cane and walking slowly, she caught the eye of every male nearby.

He took her arm in a possessive hold and they walked to the entrance of the hotel.

Once inside the hotel they crossed the lobby to the elevators. His mother had given him the room number this afternoon just before she got into the car. He kept pace with Sherri until they reached the elevator. Once it opened, Sherri stepped inside while Greg held the door for her.

He pushed the top button on the elevator and they rode up in silence. Why had his parents really come? Despite his mother's comments, he knew that his father never did anything he didn't want to do. He also knew that his father generally ignored his mother. So why cater to her whims now?

The elevator doors opened silently and they stepped into the hallway. There were only four doors on this level. Greg walked over to one and pushed a buzzer. Sherri had joined him by the time the door opened.

"Hello, Gregory," his mother said. "Please come in."

He motioned for Sherri to precede him inside.

"Hello, Mother Hogan," Sherri said with a smile. "I hope we didn't keep you waiting."

His mother didn't respond to the smile. She looked at Greg. "Penelope won't be joining us this evening," she said with barely concealed irritation. "She came down with a beastly headache and decided to stay here while we go out."

"Sorry to hear that," Greg said, suitably solemn.

"Yes, well," his mother said, turning away from them and leading them into a large room with a view of downtown Austin and the hills west of the city. "Max. Gregory is here." Since his father had already stood, her remark was unnecessary.

The four of them left the suite and took the elevator down to the lobby. Greg spotted the limo waiting for them near the entrance of the hotel.

His mother made a few remarks during the ride to the restaurant…about the weather—*beastly*—about Austin—*too provincial*—before she inquired about his job.

"It's fine," he replied tersely.

"Well, if you insist on doing police work instead of working with the company as in-house counsel, there's no reason in the world that you need to stay here in Texas." Her tone made her feelings about the state perfectly clear. "I'm certain that with your father's connections he could find you something back east."

He limited his reply to "I like living here."

Finally, his mother gave up and the four of them spent the rest of the ride in silence.

The limo pulled up in front of the restaurant. Once again Greg assisted Sherri out of the car while the driver assisted Katrina.

Max spoke to the chauffeur for a few minutes and then strode into the restaurant, Katrina hurrying to catch up with him.

"Do I have my cloak of invisibility on tonight?" Sherri asked in a low voice as she and Greg moved toward the entrance.

"Mother hopes that if she ignores you, you'll go away. You're standing in the way of her big plans."

"Then why don't you tell her the truth and call a taxi for me?"

"That would play right into her hands."

"So what? You're a big boy, Greg. You don't need me to protect you."

He almost smiled. "You're here so that my father and I don't create a brawl in a public place."

"Of course you're kidding," she said as he held the door open for her.

"Not in the least. I despise the man. The feeling is mutual."

"Okay. You've made that quite clear. What I don't understand is the fact that you've acted for years as though you had no family. Lots of people don't care for their relatives, but most don't erase them from their life."

The maître d' led the way to a corner table with Max and Katrina following behind him.

"Perhaps we could have this conversation at some other time," he said pleasantly and stepped back so that she could follow his parents.

Once seated, the four ordered drinks and studied the menu in silence. Greg glanced at his watch. He didn't want to wish anyone ill, but a call from the station about a new case would certainly be appreciated.

After they gave their orders to the waiter, Katrina turned to Greg and said, "I must say that I'm very disappointed you chose not to tell us that you were getting married. To think that you've been married for five years and I knew nothing about it! I really don't understand you at all, Greg. Why have you so stubbornly cut yourself off from your family?"

Greg took a swallow of his mixed drink, wishing he'd ordered beer, before answering her. "I don't think this is the venue in which to discuss my errant behavior, Mother."

Katrina looked at Max. "Can't you say something?" she asked in irritation.

Max had been gazing out the window until she spoke to him. He turned his head and looked at her. "Exactly what is it you expect me to say? You wanted to see Gregory. I brought you to see him. What more do you want from me?"

"He's our son! You treat him as though he were a stranger."

Max glanced at Greg for a moment. "I'm well aware of that, Katrina." With a half smile directed at Sherri, he added, "Although he looks just like I did at his age. Hardly a stranger."

Greg was relieved when their salads arrived.

His father had taken control of Greg's life at an early age. Because he wanted his father's approval so desperately, Greg followed his father's plans for him step by step. He'd gone to prep school. He'd spent three summers in Europe, learning languages and becoming familiar with other cultures. He'd graduated with honors from Harvard. He'd gotten his law degree and passed the state Bar. Then, he'd gone to work for his father.

Something happened to Greg when Max told him that he hoped to have Greg run for a political office in the state legislature once he had a little more seasoning. Greg had to face the fact that he wasn't living *his* life at all.

His escapes to Austin and Millie had been the only times when he'd truly been himself. Max had made no effort to hide his ambitions for his son. Max had money and power and having a son in politics would give him even more power. Greg knew that if he continued following his father's plans for him his father would control his entire life.

He'd been his father's puppet for most of his life and Max was only getting started.

He would never forget the day he'd told his father that he didn't intend to work for him anymore. That he had applied for a place at a prestigious police academy. He'd known his father would be upset with him and had braced himself to counter anything Max said to him.

He'd been the dutiful son all his life because he'd wanted his father to be proud of him. He'd always known that Max was grooming him to run his company.

The problem was that he didn't like the way his dad did business. His ruthlessness in acquiring assets and closing businesses without regard to the people who lost their jobs because of him was too brutal for Greg to stomach.

That meeting had opened his eyes to what his father was really like. He had viciously turned on Greg with such a personal attack that Greg felt he'd been annihilated. His blistering attack had caught Greg completely off guard. The names he'd called him and the threats he'd made to see that

Greg never had a decent job again had destroyed Greg's illusions about his father's feelings for him.

Greg hadn't seen it coming and knew he could never be a part of this family again. The man in a rage before him was contemptible in Greg's eyes.

He remembered turning around and walking out of the office with Max's words ringing in his ears. "You're no son of mine and you'll never get a cent of my money."

The lesson Greg had learned from that long-ago day was that his father had never seen him as anything more than his clone. Max had never bothered to get to know him. His father had certainly never loved him.

When Greg tried to explain to his mother why he was leaving she'd just looked at him in shock and said that of course he would do what his father wanted. It was his duty to honor his father.

Greg knew better than to continue any discussion with her.

He'd left soon afterward, and this was the first time he'd seen his family since. They hadn't even bothered to come to Millie's funeral.

After graduating from the police academy, Greg had accepted an offer to work in Austin as a chance to start over and to begin to live his own life. By the time he'd met Sherri, he'd put his family behind him. In his world, he didn't have family…except for his great-grandmother.

It was true that Sherri had asked him questions about his family but he'd put her off, not wanting to dredge up old memories. Now he was face-to-face with those memories and he knew that they had never faded.

During the course of the meal his mother did her best to keep polite conversation going, but she eventually accepted that the dinner meeting wasn't a success. After dinner they returned to the hotel and Greg signaled to have his car brought around.

"Would you like to come up for coffee?" his mother asked, making a last-ditch effort.

"Sorry," he said, helping Sherri into his car when it arrived. "Thanks for dinner." He gazed at his father. "Have a safe flight back home," he said, and walked around the car to get in.

When they pulled out of the driveway, Sherri looked over at him and said, "I don't know who you are tonight. You're definitely not the man I fell in love with and married. I have never seen anyone be so rude."

"That's why you left, wasn't it? You said I was like a stranger to you. So now you know the truth about me. I am an ungrateful son and I have no desire to spend any time with my parents. Or with Penelope. Or get involved in their lives. I have my reasons and I can live with them. You made the right choice, you know, about leaving. I'm not cut out for marriage, as you so firmly pointed out."

He pulled into the driveway of his home and drove around the house to the garage. He helped Sherri out of the car and followed her into the house. She continued through the house to the front hallway before she stopped, turned and faced him.

"Here's what I think. I think I knew parts of you better than you know yourself. You have a kind and gentle heart. You're full of compassion. You've rescued me during two very traumatic events in my life. You've been there for me. Whatever is going on between you and your father must have hurt you deeply for you to insist on locking all of your previous life away." She paused and just looked at him. "I can't help but pity you, Greg. You keep yourself bottled up so that no one can get close to you and yes, I gave up trying."

She turned and went into her room, quietly closing the door behind her.

Greg stood there for several minutes after the door closed.

He couldn't have been more shaken if she'd hit him with a two-by-four. She felt sorry for him! Why? Because he chose to live the life he wanted to live? To work in a profession that he enjoyed?

Okay. So he lived alone. Big deal. Everything worked out the way it needed to. He'd hated feeling so vulnerable where Sherri was concerned. He'd fallen in love for the first time in his life and he hadn't known how to handle it. He wasn't very good at compromise.

As though he heard a voice inside him, the thought came to him that he was, in fact, just like his father.

Sixteen

Six weeks later

Sherri heard her phone ringing as she put the key into the lock of her apartment. Whoever it was would have to wait until she got there. She didn't hurry for anyone. After getting the door open, she moved inside and closed the door behind her. She picked up the phone and said hello.

"Sherri? This is Greg."

Darn it, after she'd spent weeks dealing with her feelings for him and determinedly putting him out of her mind, he called.

"Hello, Greg."

"I was wondering if you'd have dinner with me tonight."

She took the phone away from her ear and looked at it. Finally, she said, "Why? Is this be-kind-to-your-ex week?"

He chuckled. "I don't know. If it isn't, maybe we can start a new trend. I'd like to see you."

She sighed. "Look, Greg, I know it got a little messy at the end of my stay with you and I apologize for the things I said. Your relationship with your parents is none of my business. Our pretending to be married was your idea and I went along with it, but we don't have to pretend to be friends."

"I don't want to be friends."

"Great. Look, I've got to go. I just got home and—"

"I've been doing a lot of soul-searching recently and there are some things I want to share with you."

She frowned. "Is this really Greg Hogan?"

"Oh, yeah."

"Did someone put you up to this? Is there a bet going or something?"

"Why are you surprised that I want to see you again? There's so much I want to say to you and I'd really like to talk to you in person. How about it? Will you have dinner with me tonight?"

She closed her eyes. She could see that if she said yes, she'd be putting her heart at risk again. "I don't think that's a good idea, Greg."

He didn't say anything right away. In fact, she thought he might have hung up. Finally, he said, "I really need to see you, Sherri." His voice barely audible.

Greg Hogan had never needed anything from anybody. He'd made that clear years ago. She couldn't help but be intrigued. Against her better judgment she finally replied. "All right. Where shall I meet you?"

"I'll pick you up at seven."

Not a good idea but she wasn't going to argue. "Seven," she repeated. "I'll see you then. Bye."

She hung up before her trembling became apparent in her voice. She had just agreed to do something that she knew was against her best interests. What was it about Greg that made her so weak-willed?

She had to be completely out of her mind.

Moving out of Greg's home had been as painful for her this time as it had been when they were married. Pretending to be his wife had come way too easily. She seemed to be jumping back into the fire without her asbestos suit.

She shook her head at her own foolishness. When would she ever get to the point where she could say no to Greg? Obviously not today.

Sherri went into her bedroom to find something to wear.

Greg arrived a few minutes before seven. Sherri had picked up the phone more than once to cancel the date. She would punch three or four numbers in before she'd hang up, feeling cowardly.

Now he was here. She went over and opened the door. Did he have to look so blasted masculine and mouthwateringly attractive? She would have to treat tonight as though it was routine to have a date with her ex-husband.

He nodded and offered a lopsided smile. "Hi," he said quietly. "Thank you for accepting my invitation."

"You're welcome. Come in."

He stepped inside and looked around. "Nice place. Looks comfortable. I like what you've done with it." He stuck his hands in his pockets and wandered around the room, looking at pictures on the wall. "Much nicer than the one you had when we first met."

He turned and faced her. "Do you like your new job?" he asked.

She'd never seen Greg so nervous before. "Very much."

"You're looking great, by the way."

The look he gave her was scorching. "Thank you." What had she gotten herself into? This man was not the Greg she remembered. He was far from at ease. Sherri still stood near the apartment door, watching him.

He cleared his throat. "Would you please relax? I'm not going to jump you. I would never do anything to you that you didn't want me to do. Surely you know that."

And that was her problem. After being around him this past summer, what ran through her mind was how often her dreams were filled with him making love to her. She hadn't needed the reminder.

"I know," she said slowly.

"Well," he said with a roll of his shoulders, "guess we'd better go."

He held the car door open for her. When he got into the car, he said, "Your leg seems to be fine."

"It still aches from time to time. It's more accurate than the weatherman at predicting a change."

"And your arm?"

"Good as new."

"I'm glad to hear it."

Sherri wasn't sure which one of them was more tense. She felt awkward around him now. On edge. She couldn't imagine how she would be able to eat a thing at dinner.

Once they were seated at the restaurant, Sherri felt a little better. A glass of wine helped. She ordered a salad and hoped she could eat it. Greg's appetite seemed unimpaired to judge by the meal he ordered.

When the silence between them got on her nerves, Sherri asked, "How's work? Still keeping busy?"

"Unfortunately, yes."

"How are Hannah and Sven?"

"Great."

They lapsed into silence once again.

She should have followed her instincts and canceled. Once their meals arrived, she set out to eat as quickly as possible so they could leave.

Greg asked for coffee for them once they finished eating. After the waiter brought their order, he picked up his spoon and turned it over a couple of times before nervously placing it on the table.

"I just want to say," he began and paused to clear his throat. "You didn't have to apologize for what you said about my relationship with my parents."

"Oh?"

"Yeah. Like I told you on the phone, I've done quite a bit of thinking about that situation as well as what happened to our marriage. I finally concluded that I needed to tell you some of the things I've faced about myself."

Sherri waited. His nervousness was contagious.

"It was a blow to me when I realized that I had treated you in the same way my father had treated his family. I've never heard him talk about his life before he married Mother. When I was in my early teens I asked my mother about him and she told me stories about their early marriage. She said that he'd become obsessed with making more and more money. Another time she commented that he was more comfortable in a work environment than he was in dealing with personal relationships. She said that he'd always been the kind of person who knew what he wanted and went about getting it. She'd been someone he'd wanted and he'd pursued her until she agreed to marry him."

He stopped talking and just looked at her. Sherri was blown away by his telling her all of this. She'd never heard him even touch on anything about his past.

When she didn't say anything, he said, "Does any of this sound familiar?"

"You mean because we'd known each other only a few weeks when you wanted to get married?"

"Yes."

"I suppose. So you think there's a pattern here?"

"A big one. I treated you the way he treats Mother. Even when he was home his mind was on his business. Mother learned to cope and chose to stay with him. You chose a different course."

She refused to feel guilty about her decision to end the marriage. "Yes, I did. I came to the realization that nothing was going to change between us. You had withdrawn into your work to the point where I decided that living alone was preferable to being married and being alone—emotionally, if not physically."

He nodded. "I can understand that. I guess what I wanted to tell you is that I have recognized that the very things I dislike most about my father are the traits I share with him."

What a revelation that was. She'd had no idea because she'd had no way of knowing the similarities between the two of them. Would it have made a difference in her decision? She would never know. At least Greg had been willing to share his epiphany with her now.

Knowing how much he hated his father, she knew that this realization was quite a blow to him. Impulsively she reached over and touched his hand. "That must have been hard to face."

He turned his palm up and grasped her fingers. "Yes, it was. All this time I've been feeling self-righteous and judgmental toward him. I've seen myself as standing up for what was right and going my own way."

"I take it he didn't want you to go into law enforcement."

"That's a part of it. Mostly, he wanted to be the one in control of my life. When I said no, he washed his hands of me. My father doesn't believe in making compromises."

"And neither do you?" she asked.

"Correct. When you told me the reasons you left me, I could have made changes and opened up to you then, but I didn't."

"And yet, you're telling me this now. Why?"

"Because I've been an absolute idiot where you're concerned and I miss you so much, I can barely function. I've slept in your room a few times since you left in an effort to feel closer to you. What I'm asking is whether there's a snowball's chance in hell that you might be willing for us to start over?"

No, oh, no. I can't go there again. It's too painful. Please don't ask me. Her heart beat heavily in her chest. Her fear of the pain she would feel if they tried to work it out and failed scared her to death.

Greg was watching her intently. "I remember you once said that all my past experiences had made me who I am today. I don't like myself all that much. I lost the woman I love more than anything else because I was too stiff-necked to realize what I was doing to our relationship." He looked away from her. When he looked back at her, his jaw had tightened. "I owe you so many apologies that I don't know where to start." He looked at their entwined fingers before adding, "I love you, Sherri Masterson. I never stopped loving you. And yet I did everything wrong when we were married."

She frowned. "That's not true. There were two people in the marriage, Greg. I was dealing with a lot of issues, too—the sense of abandonment was a major one. I had lost the people I loved most in the world and felt that I had lost you in all the ways that mattered, as well. A lot of my buttons were being pushed."

"Thank you for hearing me out this evening. You could have gotten up and left and I would have understood. But you didn't, and I appreciate your patience more than I can say. Do you think it's possible that we might be able to work things out?"

She stared into his eyes, knowing that this was the fork in the road of her life. Risk everything in hopes of gaining everything?

Finally, Sherri nodded. "I'd like to think so, yes." She smiled tentatively at him.

"I do have one other request to make."

She eyed him suspiciously. "And what is that?"

"Will you go to Connecticut with me? I want to go see my parents."

Seventeen

Sherri stared at him as though he'd started speaking in a foreign language. And maybe he had. Opening up to Sherri and enumerating his many faults had been the toughest thing he'd ever done in his life.

"You don't need me, Greg. You know that."

"Yes, I do know that. It isn't a question of need. I'm going to want your support if you're willing to give it. I have no idea how the visit will turn out."

"When are you planning to go?"

"Whenever you say."

"I can't ask for time off. I haven't worked there long enough."

"Okay. Then we'll do it on a weekend. Fly up Friday, come back Sunday."

"You're serious about doing this."

"Very."

"Let me think about it, okay?"

The waiter brought their check. Greg gave him his credit card and they waited while the waiter rang it up.

He couldn't keep his eyes off Sherri. Her hair had grown out some and she'd had it trimmed since he'd last seen her. Now it curved around her face, framing it.

After the waiter returned, Greg took Sherri's hand and they walked to his car. At least she hadn't said no. She'd given him hope, and he was determined to do everything he could to convince her that the two of them could make it.

He turned into the driveway of the apartment complex where she lived. "Did you get another car?"

"Not yet. I'm on one of the bus routes until I decide what I want. As much as I loved my little car, I want something larger—steel-plated, perhaps."

"I can understand that." They arrived at her door and he waited for her to unlock it. When the door opened, Sherri looked at him and said, "Would you like to come in for more coffee?"

He breathed deeply, not certain how to handle her invitation. Finally, he said, "I would very much like to come inside, but it won't be because I want coffee."

She nodded and went into her apartment. When she didn't say anything he knew that he was pushing a little too hard.

She turned and looked at him for a long moment. *Okay, here it comes.*

"Please come in, Greg," she said softly, a slight smile on her face.

She didn't have to ask him twice.

As soon as he stepped inside and closed the door behind them, he grabbed her and kissed her the way he'd been wanting to since the moment he'd first seen her tonight. He couldn't touch her enough, sliding his hand down her side and catching her knee. She responded by clutching his shoulders and hotly kissing him back.

He'd wanted her for too long not to know he wasn't going to last. He lifted her, turned and leaned her against the door, his hands feeling for her panties. She was moist and hot and he couldn't wait any longer. He tore her panties and dropped them to the floor, reached down and unzipped himself and plunged into her, frantic to be inside her.

Greg climaxed in an embarrassingly short time, his knees shaking as he clung to her. When he could breathe again he slowly lowered her until she was standing. "I am so sorry, honey. I didn't mean to act like a caveman. I just—"

She put her fingers over his lips. "Don't apologize, please." She leaned down and scooped up her torn panties.

He'd screwed up, big-time. "Look. I'll replace them. I can't believe that I—"

"Come on. I think we'd be more comfortable without so many clothes on." She turned and led him into her bedroom.

Greg wasted no time stripping off his clothes. She was reaching for the zipper in the back of her dress when he leaned over and quickly unzipped it. She shrugged and it fell off her shoulders and pooled around her feet. She hadn't worn a bra. None of it detracted from her beauty.

She glanced down at the scar from her surgery. "Not a pretty sight, I'm afraid," she said, and he realized he'd been staring at her.

"You're beautiful. I'm so sorry you had to endure all of that."

She ignored him and ran her fingers down his chest, pausing at the juncture of his thighs, her hand stroking him. "I'm happy to see you, too, big guy," she said, and leaned over and caressed him with her tongue.

That ended all conversation. Greg attempted to make up

for the time they'd been apart, or together yet not together. He brought her to a climax more than once before he let go and made a final surge within her.

He collapsed beside her and acknowledged to himself there was no way to catch up, no matter how badly he wanted to wipe out the last two years.

He dropped off to sleep and, when he woke later, realized he'd been asleep over an hour. Sherri wasn't there but he smelled coffee and knew she must be in the other room. Greg took a quick shower and dressed before going in search of the tantalizing scent.

He found Sherri in the kitchen, wrapped in a terry-cloth robe, pouring coffee into two mugs. She heard him and turned around. "I thought you might want some coffee after all."

Greg reached for the cup, chuckling. "Thanks." He took a sip before saying, "Guess tonight's my night for apologies. Sorry I fell asleep."

She leaned against the counter and watched him while she sipped on her coffee. "I didn't mind."

He sat at the bar and said, "I'd like you to move back in with me."

She shook her head. "Thank you, but no."

"No?"

"Greg, I'm no longer the naive twenty-one-year-old jumping to do your bidding. Give me a chance to deal with all of this. When I got home this evening, the very last thing I would have thought I'd be doing was not only seeing you but ending up in bed with you. I need a little space."

He shrugged. "I'm sorry. I guess I thought that—" He waved his hand toward the bedroom.

She smiled. "That all we needed was an evening of good sex to make everything all right?"

He felt sheepish. "I suppose," he said ruefully.

"I've discovered some things about me, as well, during these past several months. I know now that in the past I've made most of my decisions with my heart instead of my head."

"And your head is telling you...what?"

"To take this slow."

He smiled. "You call the last couple of hours taking it slow? I think I broke some kind of record racing you to the finish line!"

"What happened tonight has been building up between us since you came back into my life. Both of us wanted it and both of us are consenting adults. I'm just not ready to make a commitment to you at this point. I need to deal with some things that I harbored before I can be free of them. We have time to decide what we want in the future."

"I already know."

"But you don't really know me anymore. We didn't spend much time together while I stayed with you. I think we need to get reacquainted. I'd like to get to know this new, introspective person you've become."

"I'm still the same person. And you... I know you like I know my own body."

"Exactly. Physically, you know me well. However, in other ways you don't know me at all. I tried so hard to conform to what you wanted during our marriage that I became an extension of you. I won't do that again."

He ran his hand through his hair in frustration. Of course she was right. He just hadn't wanted to say goodbye tonight. He'd wanted to go to sleep with her in his arms.

"So. What next? We continue to date and have great sex?"

She looked at him, her amusement at his impatience obvious. Then she took in a big breath and sighed. "I love you,

Greg Hogan. I always have. Leaving you was hell. Seeing you
again was sheer torture, reminding me of what I had missed
in my life. Love wasn't enough to keep us together before. I
think we need to take some time now to work out issues we
may still have...that we've never discussed before...before
we jump into something."

He finished his coffee and stood. "You're probably right,"
he finally conceded.

"Thank you for understanding."

He walked over to her and draped his arms around her. He
scattered light kisses over her face. With a mock sigh he leaned
back and looked at her. "Somehow, I feel so used. All you want
from me is sex." Her mouth dropped open and he laughed.
"Guess I needed to say that. I feel much better now." He gave
her a resounding kiss and stepped back. "See ya around, kid.
Gimme a call whenever you need a little tune-up."

"Greg!" She was fighting not to laugh. "Go home, get
some rest. As long as you understand that you're my stud-on-
call, we should get along great."

Darn woman. Always had to have the last word.

Eighteen

Greg drove home on autopilot. He'd been relieved when Sherri had agreed to have dinner with him. She'd understood how difficult it was for him to face his mistakes and admit them to her. She'd been open and compassionate with him, which he hadn't deserved but had desperately needed.

Sherri had made passionate love with him and he'd taken that as a signal that, with their new understanding, they would pick up where they'd left off in their relationship.

He'd never been more wrong. She didn't trust him. The realization had leveled him, but it wasn't the gut-wrenching pain he'd felt when she'd left him. At least she was willing to try. It gave him insight on how she must have felt when she didn't believe that he had trusted her.

He knew she was susceptible to him; she'd admitted as much. But something told him she'd resent him using her feelings for him to manipulate her into coming back to him.

You've got one chance, buster. Don't blow it.

Would he ever get enough of making love to her? He doubted that very much. So how did he handle the present situation? Somehow he didn't think she'd continue to make love to him without a commitment, one she wasn't willing to make right away, which meant...what?

He pulled into the garage and walked into the home that had seemed so empty after she'd moved out. He knew that when his parents were here, she'd been teasing him by telling them that they planned to have a family, but he was serious about having a home and children with Sherri. Even though he didn't think he'd be all that great a father—he certainly didn't want to be like *his* father—he knew that he would work at it by allowing himself to open up and love his children and, most of all, listen to them as individuals.

She'd been right. He had been closed off from her, arrogantly believing that she didn't need to know about his history with his family and why he'd cut himself off from them. So, yes, he'd withheld major parts of his life—and himself—from her.

He'd been an ass. Man, did he hate to admit that to himself. He'd been so blasted self-righteous. The consequence of his behavior was her lack of trust in him. Getting her to agree to marry him, to trust him, to believe in him, would be challenging, but he had no choice. He didn't want to spend the rest of his life without her.

Greg went upstairs to bed. Not that he expected to sleep. His thoughts would no doubt keep him awake for most of the night. He lay in the dark, his hands behind his head.

When the phone rang sometime later he immediately thought of Sherri. Was she lying awake, too?

"This is Greg," he said gruffly.

"Hello, Gregory. This is your mother."

"Well. Hello."

"I wanted to let you know that your father is in the hospital."

"What happened?"

"He was at the office talking with one of his aides when he crumpled. Thank goodness the aide stopped him from falling to the floor. They called an ambulance. I've been at the hospital all afternoon and evening. They're keeping him for the next couple of days. They want to run several tests to figure out what is going on. I just got home and thought I should notify you. I know it would be too much to ask of you to come see him, but I thought you would want to know."

"Is he conscious?"

"Oh, yes! And demanding to go home, threatening to fire whoever called the ambulance from the office."

Greg chuckled. "Sounds like everything's normal, then. As a matter of fact, Sherri and I were discussing coming to visit. She's working now and we won't be able to come until the weekend. Will that be all right?"

"Oh, Greg," Katrina said, her voice breaking. "Thank you. I know he'd be pleased to see you."

"Not a chance of that, but there are some things I want to discuss with him."

"Not if you're going to upset him. He doesn't need any more stress than what he's dealing with right now."

"Give me a little credit, okay? I'm not going to charge in there and tell him off."

"Well, since you haven't spoken to him in years, you may forgive me for my concerns."

Greg paused, trying to think of something to reassure his mother regarding his motives. Finally, he said, "I'd really like to see him."

"Shall I send someone to meet you at the airport?"

"No. I'll rent a car. We'll be in either late Friday or Saturday morning." He could only hope Sherri would be willing to go with him such a short time after he'd asked her.

"Well." His mother hesitated. "Just in case you decide not to come, I'll not mention the possibility of your visit to your father."

He grinned. The truth was that his mother didn't want to deal with his father's reaction to the idea of Greg showing up. He had no doubt that his father would not want to see him.

"Thanks for calling. I'll be in touch."

The persistent sound of a phone ringing somewhere nearby finally brought Sherri out of a deep sleep. She fumbled for the phone without bothering to turn on a light.

"H'lo?"

There was only silence.

Figured. It was either a wrong number or a crank call. "Hello?" she said again, ready to hang up.

"My timing stinks, I know. I'll call back in the morning," Greg said.

She sat up in bed. "Greg? Why are you calling?"

Again, there was silence. Finally, he said with obvious reluctance, "Do you remember the favor I asked from you at dinner?"

"We talked about a lot of things, Greg."

"About visiting my family."

"Oh. Yes. Do I have to decide tonight?"

"My mother called just now to say my father is in the hospital."

"Oh, no! What's wrong? Is he going to be okay?"

"They're running tests to find out. I told her I'd be up there this weekend. I'm hoping you'll go with me."

She dropped back onto her pillow. She was more than half-asleep and he wanted an answer *now?*

She sighed. She'd led such a calm, simple life before her accident. She'd felt in control of her life, content with her home, her job, her very existence. The only constant in her life since then was Lucifer, who at the moment was making it clear that his sleep had been disturbed and that he was far from happy.

She rubbed her forehead.

"Sherri? You still there?"

Oh, to heck with it. One more opportunity to learn more about Greg. "I'm here. And yes, if we can leave after work on Friday, I'll go."

He made no effort to disguise his sigh of relief. "I'll make the arrangements and call you with the information tomorrow."

"'Night, Greg."

"Thanks, Sherri. Go back to sleep."

She hung up the phone and did just that.

As soon as they left the airport on Saturday morning and headed toward Greg's former home, Sherri felt as though she'd stepped into another universe. She'd never visited the northeast before. It was nothing like Texas.

She gazed at the scenery and, after a while, at the homes. They were huge and each sat in solitary splendor. She couldn't imagine living in a home that could double as a hotel.

Greg slowed and turned into the driveway of one of those homes. The landscaping added to the overall sense of stately living and old money.

"How old is the house?"

"At least a hundred years. It was my mother's family home. Millie grew up here and lived here until she married. The family updated it periodically, adding all the latest conveniences."

"I thought your father might have bought it."

"Not a chance. He definitely married into money and never looked back."

"So your parents' marriage wasn't a love match?"

"It was definitely a love match as far as Mother was concerned. Who knows what Father thought or felt." He stopped in front of steps leading to the front door. "So. Here we are."

"How long has it been since you've been here?"

"Since I went into the police academy."

"You really were angry."

"I suppose. As far as I know, my father disinherited me once I left."

"You don't know?"

"I know my father. He never threatens…he acts. He said I'd never get another cent of his money. I believe him."

Sherri couldn't understand a family like that. She would have given everything to have her parents still alive. There was no way she could have gone so long without seeing them.

"How sad," she finally said.

He got out of the car and went around to open the door for her. He helped her out and said, "I suppose. I was just relieved to be out from under his thumb."

Once at the door, Greg rang the bell. When the door opened, he broke into a big grin. "Hello, Maribeth. How's my favorite girl?" He hugged the slim, elderly woman and gave her a smacking kiss on the cheek.

She stared at him as though seeing a ghost. "Gregory?"

"In the flesh."

"Come in, come in. No sense standing here with the door open. I can't believe my eyes," she said, closing the door behind them. While the two chatted, Sherri took the opportunity to survey her surroundings. The foyer was triple the size of the one in Greg's home, with priceless artwork hanging on the walls and sculptures on pedestals.

Greg said, "Forgive my manners, Maribeth. This is my wife, Sherri. Sherri, Maribeth practically raised me." He looked back at the older woman. "I am so glad to know you're still here."

"Where else would I be? My family has worked for yours for years and years. My granddaughter started working here in the kitchen just last summer."

"Amazing," Greg replied.

"Come. Your mother and father are in the dining room, having breakfast. Would you like something?"

"I'd love to have breakfast and lots of coffee. How about you?" he asked Sherri, hugging her to him.

He appeared comfortable pretending they were still married. She wished she could feel the same. "Yes, thank you."

"I'll get it ready," Maribeth said. "I believe you know where to find the dining room."

"I'll manage somehow." Greg took Sherri's hand. "Ready?"

"I suppose." She knew he recognized her reluctance.

He led her toward the back of the foyer and turned down a hallway. She'd better start leaving bread crumbs behind in order not to get lost. At last he came to a swinging door and pushed it open.

"Oh, good. Maribeth, could you bring us some—"

Katrina had her back to the door and only saw them as they came farther into the room.

"Dear God!" Max said. "I must be dying. Why else would you show up?"

"Nonsense, Max," Katrina replied. "Can't your oldest son come to visit you without a reason?"

"No." He pushed back his chair and stood. Greg walked over

to him and they shook hands. It was definitely a Kodak moment. "Sit down and have some breakfast," Max said. "I'll ring Maribeth and have her—"

"She's already on it. She answered the door when we arrived."

"Didn't hear the damn thing. My hearing must be going."

Sherri had been taking in the room. The place could be a museum. The table could comfortably seat five on each side and yet Max and Katrina sat at opposite ends of the table. They probably used cell phones to communicate with each other.

Sherri sat next to Greg, near his mother.

"The cast is gone from your leg," Katrina said, stating the obvious.

"Yes."

"Well…I'm glad to see you're well again."

Maribeth came in with two steaming plates and a large carafe of coffee on a tray.

She set the plates in front of them, placed the cups on the table and filled them with coffee. "Is there anything else you need?"

While Greg said no, Sherri stared at her plate in dismay. She could use a hollow leg or an additional stomach if she was expected to eat everything on the platter in front of her.

She had a choice of scrambled eggs, bacon, sausage, ham, hash browns and French toast.

Sherri glanced at Greg, who was eating from his similar plate with a great deal of gusto. She looked at Katrina's plate and saw that she had been eating toast and fruit. Did Maribeth think she was a lumberjack?

Sherri picked up her fork and made a valiant effort to eat as much as she could.

After breakfast, the four of them went into a room that was beautifully decorated and yet looked lived-in. Sherri hadn't realized that she'd literally been holding her breath until her chest hurt. She hurriedly exhaled.

Katrina and Max claimed matching recliners and she and Greg sat on the sofa across from them. There was a huge plasma television hanging on one of the walls. A basket of knitting sat beside Katrina's chair. She reached into the basket and pulled out her knitting. Her hands stayed busy as Max said, "Don't mean to sound rude, but why, after all these years, did you decide to come back here? Oh. Wait. Katrina called you, didn't she?"

"Yes, Mother called me but we were already planning to come. We just moved the trip up."

"All right. You're here. Now tell me why."

Sherri waited with the other three to hear Greg's answer.

Greg leaned forward, propping his elbows on his knees. "I've been doing a lot of thinking since you were in Austin. I took a hard look at myself and discovered that everything I've done to live my own life hasn't worked because I'm just like you. So wherever I am and whatever I do, you're there. I figured since that was the case, I might want to get to know you better."

Max stared at him in surprise. He looked at Katrina. "I'm not certain, but I think I've just been insulted."

Katrina rolled her eyes. "He's your son, Max. Of course he's just like you. He always has been. I have no doubt that he's a workaholic who bottles up his thoughts and emotions just like you, that he's got to control everything around him and that he keeps himself aloof from the world."

Max looked from Katrina to Greg. "Did you two plan this?"

Greg shook his head. He smiled. "Like it or not, we're very much alike. To dislike you means I dislike myself. I set out to be the exact opposite of you. Instead, I became you." He grinned at Max.

"Well, hell. I don't know what to think. You'd think if we were alike, we'd get along."

"We did. Until I became an adult and decided I didn't want the life you'd planned for me."

"Kyle didn't mind taking your place."

"Then you should be happy."

Max shrugged. "I'm always happy." He sat there wearing his perpetual scowl.

Greg laughed and before long Katrina joined him. As amused as Sherri was, she didn't want him to think she was laughing at him.

"Have you looked into a mirror recently?" Greg asked.

The corners of Max's mouth lifted. "Not if I can avoid it."

"Take my word for it. You look far from happy. I'm here because I need to know you better without wearing filters from the past."

"Humph."

"So…Sherri and I plan to spend the day and night with you and fly back to Austin tomorrow afternoon."

Max raised his eyebrows. "Well, well. I dare say it will be an interesting weekend."

"So what's the deal with your health?"

"There's not a blasted thing wrong with me."

"Actually," Katrina said calmly, "that isn't true, but we'll leave that alone for now. Just enjoy your time together."

Nineteen

Sherri was asleep when Greg slipped into bed with her late that night. His cold hands and feet immediately woke her.

"Hey! Your hands are freezing."

"I know. I thought you'd take pity on me and get me warm."

She turned to face him. "Was this your room growing up?" She couldn't see his expression in the dark. "Probably."

"You mean you don't know?"

"I wasn't paying any attention. Do you have any idea how many bedrooms there are in the place?"

"At least eight."

"At least." He pulled her closer and nibbled on her ear.

Sherri had known before they left Austin that they would probably be sharing a room this weekend. She had tried not to think about it, but it was obvious that Greg had making love to her very much on his mind.

Her thoughts scattered when he kissed her. When he

paused for a moment, he said, "I feel wicked having sex in my parents' home with someone I'm not married to." He kissed her again. "Deliciously wicked."

"I'm sure you've had sex many times when you weren't married."

"Not here and not since we broke up."

She stilled. "Are you saying you haven't made love to anyone since the divorce?"

"I didn't say I was proud of it. It's just a fact. How about you? Or am I being much too personal?"

"I haven't been on a *date* since our divorce, much less hopped into bed with anyone."

He kissed her again, a long, drugging kiss. "I'm glad," he whispered when they finally paused for air. "I want this to work between us this time. I'll do whatever I have to do to make it work."

He cupped her breast and groaned. "You always have too many clothes on when we're in bed," he grumbled. One of his familiar complaints when they'd been married. He'd wanted her to sleep in the nude, but it was hard to break a habit of a lifetime.

She sat up and pulled her gown over her head before stretching out beside him.

"Mmm. Much better." He tugged on one of her nipples with his mouth. "Much, much better. You taste so sweet."

She couldn't lie still. She moved against him, brushing against his erection. With a deft move he slid her beneath him and entered her in one long surge. She groaned with pleasure.

"Did I hurt you? Am I rushing things?"

"No and no." She held on to him as he set a slow, steady rhythm, taking his time and driving her crazy. She met each thrust, wanting him so badly she thought she'd die from it.

Toward the end he stepped up the pace and they reached a

climax at the same time. Clutching each other, they rode the pleasurable sensations until their hearts stopped racing.

Sherri thought Greg had fallen to sleep when he said, "I'm glad we made the trip."

"How did things go with your father?"

"Better than I expected. I'm sorry I didn't spend more time with you today."

"Now that would have been silly, since you specifically made the trip to talk with him."

"Did Mother entertain you?"

Sherri was grateful for the dark. She didn't want Greg to see her grinning. "Why, yes, she was the perfect hostess. She showed me around the house and gave me the history of it. We did a tour of the gardens and she told me how old they were and…" Wasn't that enough?

"And what?"

"Oh, she told me all about her plans for you to marry one of the debutantes in her circle and made it subtly clear that I didn't deserve you."

He groaned. "Do you want me to say something to her?"

She laughed. She couldn't help it. "Greg. Your mother made it clear how she felt about me in your life when she first met me."

"I don't want her being rude to you."

"She wasn't. She was the personification of the great lady dealing with a member of the lower class. It was all I could do not to laugh."

"You weren't offended?"

"How could I be? She's an absolute stereotype of a person born into privilege and wealth. Almost a caricature, come to think of it. I can't imagine you having a mother like that."

"I saw very little of her when I was a child. Maribeth raised me, doing her best to turn me into something resembling a gentleman. I barely knew my mother. She was the lady who flitted in and out of my life, absently patting me on the head whenever she happened to run across me."

"Greg! That's awful."

"It was normal to me."

"So her opinion of me doesn't make a difference to you?"

"Are you kidding? Now, Maribeth not liking you would have given me pause. Fortunately for any future we might have together, Maribeth thought I'd made an excellent choice. She said she was so pleased that I'd ignored the overbred young ladies Mother tried so hard to foist on me. Her word— *foist*. I thought it rather apt."

Sherri settled her head on his shoulder. "Then the trip has been a success for you," she said, yawning. "Good."

"Having you with me was the best part."

The following Monday was a typical day at the office. Sherri considered it more on the level of controlled chaos. She ignored it and focused on her writing.

One of the women who worked there stopped by her desk that afternoon. "You're certainly cheerful today, considering it's a Monday. You must have had a great weekend."

"I did."

"What did you do?"

"Flew to Connecticut with my ex-husband to see his parents."

The woman's jaw dropped. "That's your idea of fun? My idea of a fun time with my ex would be watching him being washed away by a tidal wave." She looked at Sherri more closely. "I didn't know you were divorced."

"I am."

"And you're spending time with your ex? Doesn't that sort of defeat the purpose of getting the divorce?"

"Probably, but I always believe in second chances...for every-body."

"Better you than me, honey. I'm thrilled at the idea that I will never have to see my ex again." She gave Sherri a little wave and left.

The thing was, Greg was no longer the man she'd been married to. If nothing else, the weekend had changed him in some indefinable way. His father didn't seem any different to her. Whatever he and Greg talked about would be between them, but Greg acted as though a weight had been lifted from his shoulders.

He'd been in a teasing mood all the way back to Austin and she'd laughed more than she had in years. He'd taken her back to her apartment, given her a smacking kiss and told her he'd call her sometime today.

He'd been happier than she'd ever seen him. She was pleased for him.

When Sherri left the building a week later she saw Greg waiting for her in the parking lot. He was leaning against his car in a familiar pose and wearing his leather jacket with the fur collar turned up. As soon as he saw her he started toward her.

Some woman behind her said, "Boy oh boy, would I like some hunk to be looking at *me* that way!"

As soon as he reached her side, he gave her a bear hug and said, "I thought I'd give you a ride home. Save you standing out in the wind and cold waiting for a bus."

She smiled up at him, feeling a surge of love for him that she'd once thought would never return. "Thank you."

"I also have Hannah making dinner for two tonight. How does that sound?"

"I like it. No cooking for me tonight."

He hustled her to the car and carefully closed the door behind her before getting inside.

"Mmm. The car is warm."

He looked over at her and smiled. "I planned it that way."

"If I didn't know better, I'd think you were planning to seduce me later."

"My intentions are much more honorable."

"That's good to know."

He leaned over and lifted her chin slightly and kissed her...a slow, sweet, heartwarming gesture that made no demands.

She sighed when he pulled away. "And hello to you, too."

He laughed. "Do you need to go by your apartment first?"

She thought for a minute. "Well, I need to feed Lucifer. Otherwise, he'll give me nothing but trouble when I get home later."

"It's the darnedest thing, but I actually miss that cat," he said, pulling into the street.

"No way."

"I know. Surprises me. I don't seem to be allergic to him. He's got a distinct personality all his own."

"Without a doubt."

"So we'll go by and feed him and then go to my place."

They were greeted at the door with a litany of complaints about the weather, the dog in the next apartment and the fact that Lucifer's food bowl was empty.

Greg leaned against the counter with his feet crossed and arms folded, watching her routine with her furry feline friend. Once she'd fed him, she said, "As you can see, I'm no longer important in his life. He probably won't notice I've left."

At Greg's home, Hannah greeted her with pleasure, commenting on how well she'd healed since the summer.

Greg asked Sherri, "Care for a glass of wine before dinner?"

"Sounds good." They took their drinks into the den, which

had a cozy fire going. "Everything looks so different here in the winter."

"I like coming home to it, winter or summer."

"I can certainly understand that."

They sat in the two high-backed chairs in front of the fireplace. Greg knew her favorite wine. Let's face it, he knew more about her than any other living human being. She found that almost comforting.

"How are things at work?" she asked after they'd sat staring into the fire for a while. If they didn't start talking, she was going to fall asleep right there.

He smiled. "My boss got transferred today so all is right with my little world."

"You didn't like him very much, did you?"

"Actually, it was the other way around. He thinks his suspicions have been confirmed—I'm really after his job."

"Are you?"

"Absolutely not. I like my job."

"So who will be your next boss?"

He shrugged. "Who knows? I don't really care. I do what I do and I'm good at it. Most people would be pleased to have someone like that working for them."

Hannah appeared in the doorway. "Dinner is ready."

Greg stood and offered his hand to Sherri. "Shall we?"

He led her into the dining room and the alcove where they usually ate. Candles sparkled and were reflected in the windows. "Everything looks so nice, Hannah," Sherri said.

"Thank you."

She served soup and later salad before bringing out their main course.

"I hadn't realized how hungry I was until I smelled the succulent roast beef," she said to Greg. "The woman is amazing."

"That she is." He picked up the bottle of wine and refilled their glasses. Handing Sherri her glass, he said, "I propose a toast."

"Sounds good." She touched the rim of her glass to his.

"To your continued good health and to us," he said.

She looked into his gorgeous eyes that reflected the candle-light and said, "Thank you," and took a sip of her wine.

By the time they finished dinner Sherri was full and relaxed. Hannah cleared the table and brought them each a small cup of crème brûlée and coffee.

"I'm not sure I can eat another bite."

"There's not much there. Eat whatever you want."

She ate the dessert and groaned with pleasure. When she finished, she reached for her cup of coffee.

"Sherri, do you remember leaving your wedding rings on the kitchen counter the day you left?"

She dropped her hand to the table. "I remember everything about that day."

"You'd put them in the box they came in and I almost tossed it away, thinking it was empty."

She could think of nothing to say.

"I wanted to start over completely with you." He pulled out a small box. "I hope you like it."

Sherri took the box, her hand trembling. She opened it and tears filled her eyes.

The ring was a vividly green emerald surrounded by diamonds. "I wanted to match your eyes," he said quietly.

She looked at him, the tears running down her cheeks, and reached for his hand. "I don't know how to thank you."

"I do. Will you marry me?"

"Oh, Greg, this is so beautiful."

"I want you to have it. I hope that you'll consider it an engagement ring, but if not, I still want you to have it."

"Of course—" her voice broke "—of course I'll marry you. I can't imagine my life without you in it."

He came around the table and took her hands, pulling her up and into him. The kiss he gave her spoke to her on a deep and emotional level. When it ended, he said, "This time, we'll do it any way you want. Anywhere you want. Any month or year you want. I came close to losing you completely after the accident and I know I don't want to live on the planet without your being here, even if I never see you again." Greg's eyes were moist, as well.

She smiled. "Thank you for that. I've had an idea about how I wanted our next wedding to go, since we were married by the justice of the peace the first time."

"Whatever you want, sweetheart. Whatever you want."

Epilogue

Spring still hadn't reached New England the following April. Mother Nature had saved her most severe weather for early spring. Not that Sherri minded. The church was well-heated. Greg's sister-in-law, Marsha, had helped her dress. She would be Sherri's only attendant this morning. Kyle, Marsha's husband and Greg's brother, was his best man.

"You look like a fairy-tale princess," Marsha said. "You just glow."

"I'm happy."

"I'm glad. I didn't want Katrina's attitude toward the wedding to be upsetting to you."

"Not in the least. She's being honest and I like that in anyone."

"Do you think she'll be here?"

"I have no idea."

There was a tap on the door. "Ready?" a muffled male voice asked.

Marsha opened the door for Sherri and followed her out of the room, carefully holding her train.

Sherri looked up at Max. "This time around, I'm completely ready."

Katrina had been horrified to discover that Sherri and Greg had been divorced when she'd met Sherri. She couldn't believe their deception. So when Greg called to tell her that they would like to have their wedding in the church he'd attended growing up, she'd been incensed with him. She'd declared she would have nothing to do with any of it and she had kept her word.

"Thank you for walking me down the aisle," Sherri said, taking Max's hand.

"Thank you for asking me. I know I can never replace your father, but I have a hunch he's right here with us today."

She hugged him. "I hope so."

When it was time for her to enter, the organ music that had been playing softly in the background changed into a processional and everyone in the church stood. Sherri was amazed to see that the place was packed.

"Who are all these people?" she whispered to Max.

"Family and friends, business associates, the curious."

She nodded, even though she didn't understand. Who had contacted them about the wedding? She had thought it would be a private wedding.

She and Max walked slowly down the aisle toward Greg and Kyle. Sherri couldn't decide who had a bigger grin on his face. Both looked like Max. She couldn't help grinning back at them.

They reached the pastor and stopped. After his opening remarks and a prayer, the pastor asked who gave Sherri to Greg to be married. Max, in a stentorian voice said, "Every member of the Hogan clan, myself included."

Everyone in the congregation laughed.

The rest of the wedding went according to plan. She and Greg had written vows that were deeply personal to them, but Sherri no longer cared if others heard them. Their vows had come out of their pain and loneliness for each other after their first marriage had ended. The vows were filled with hope and new promises that they fully intended to honor and when the pastor told them that they were now legally husband and wife, and told Greg he could kiss his bride, Greg wrapped his arms around her and kissed her as though no one else was in the room.

Once again the congregation stood, laughed and applauded.

Greg turned her and faced those who were there. It was then that Sherri saw Katrina standing next to Max—who was beaming as though he'd just acquired several more companies— daintily wiping her eyes with an embroidered handkerchief.

Sherri and Greg walked back up the aisle until they reached the narthex of the church, where they were surrounded by well-wishers. Greg leaned over and whispered in her ear, "You and Mother have something in common besides marrying a Hogan. You were both pregnant brides." He gave her a wicked smile.

"Somehow I doubt that she'll be thrilled by that piece of information."

"Who cares?" He picked her up and twirled her around. "Dad's going to be happy to add another grandchild to the family."

"Dad?" she whispered.

He grinned. "He said he was tired of being called Father."

It was then that Max and Katrina walked up to greet them. Greg put Sherri back on her feet and grabbed his father's hand with both of his. "Way to go, Dad. I was proud of you."

Max's eyes danced. He nodded toward Sherri and said to Greg. "You got yourself a good one, son. Try not to screw it up again," and hugged first Greg and then Sherri. When he stepped back from her, he said, "Welcome to the family, sweetheart. If he gives you any grief, let me know and I'll straighten him out for you."

"Oh, Max," Katrina said irritably. "You're holding up the line. We'll see them at the reception."

Greg leaned over and kissed Katrina's cheek. "Be thinking up some good names for your next grandchild, Mother. We'll need them by October."

Her eyes widened. She looked at both Greg and Sherri and then at Max. "Did you know about this?" she whispered.

Max shook his head. "Not a word. Guess there was no help for it, then. Greg knew I'd horsewhip him if he didn't do right by this little lady."

Katrina suddenly looked very vulnerable. "Just like my father threatened to do to you."

Max threw his arm around her and kissed her. "What he never knew was that I would have married you whether he approved or not. Greg being on the way was the greatest thing that could have happened to us. It meant that you would marry me when I didn't have two dimes to rub together. You always said it didn't matter to you, which was another reason I was so crazy about you!"

"You were?" she repeated, sounding shaken.

Max sobered. "You mean you didn't know?"

Katrina shook her head.

Max took her hand and said to Greg, "I'll meet you two newlyweds at the reception. Don't wait for us. We may be running a little late." He turned to Katrina and said, "Come with me. I can see I need to give you some convincing of my love for you." He started walking toward the entrance of the church while Katrina, a rosy red, followed him.

Greg looked at Sherri and chuckled. "Looks like there'll be more than one couple having a second honeymoon tonight. Let's go to the reception and get something to eat. I'm starving. And I'll need all my strength for later."

As others stopped by to wish the couple well they spoke to a beaming groom and a very blushing bride.

* * * * *

Turn the page for a sneak preview
of the first book in the new miniseries
DIAMONDS DOWN UNDER
from Silhouette Desire®,
VOWS & A VENGEFUL GROOM
by Bronwyn Jameson

Available January 2008

Silhouette Desire®
Always Powerful, Passionate and Provocative

Kimberley Blackstone didn't notice the waiting horde of media until it was too late. Flashbulbs exploded around her like a New Year's light show. She skidded to a halt, so abruptly her trailing suitcase all but overtook her.

This had to be a case of mistaken identity. Surely. Kimberley hadn't been on the paparazzi hit list for close to a decade, not since she'd estranged herself from her billionaire father and his headline-hungry diamond business.

But no, it was *her* name they called. *Her* face was the focus of a swarm of lenses that circled her like avid hornets. Her heart started to pound with fear-fueled adrenaline.

What did they want?

What was going on?

With a rising sense of bewilderment she scanned the crowd for a clue, and her gaze fastened on a tall, leonine figure forcing his way to the front. A tall, familiar figure. Her head came up in stunned recognition, and their gazes collided across the sea of heads before the cameras erupted with another barrage of flashes, this time right in her exposed face.

Blinded by the flashbulbs—and by the shock of that momentary eye-meet—Kimberley didn't realize his intent until he'd forged his way to her side, possibly by the sheer strength of his personality. She felt his arm wrap around her shoulder, pulling her into the protective shelter of his body, allowing her no time to object. No chance to lift her hands to ward him off.

In the space of a hastily drawn breath, she found herself plastered knee-to-nose against six feet two inches of hard-bodied male.

Ric Perrini.

Her lover for ten torrid weeks, her husband for ten tumultuous days.

Her ex for ten tranquil years.

After all this time, he should not have felt so familiar but, oh dear, he did. She knew the scent of that body and its lean, muscular strength. She knew its heat and its slick power and every response it could draw from hers.

She also recognized the ease with which he'd taken control of the moment and the decisiveness of his deep voice when it rumbled close to her ear. "I have a car waiting outside. Is this your only luggage?"

Kimberley nodded. "I assume you will tell me," she said tightly, "what this welcome party is all about."

"Not while the welcome party is within earshot. No."

Barking a request for the cameramen to stand aside, Perrini took her hand and pulled her into step with his ground-eating stride. Kimberley let him, because he was right, damn his arrogant, Italian-suited hide. Despite the speed with which he whisked her across the airport terminal, she could almost feel the hot breath of the pursuing media on her back.

This was neither the time nor the place for explanations. Inside his car, however, she would get answers.

Now that the initial shock had been blown away—by the haste of their retreat, by the heat of her gathering indignation, by the rush of adrenaline fired by Perrini's presence and the looming verbal battle—her brain was starting to tick over. This had to be her father's doing. And if it was a Howard Blackstone publicity ploy, then it had to be about Blackstone Diamonds, the company that ruled his life.

The knowledge made her chest tighten with a familiar ache of disillusionment.

She'd known her father would be flying in from Sydney for today's opening of the newest in his chain of exclusive, high-end jewelry boutiques. The opulent shopfront sat adjacent to the rival business where Kimberley worked. No coincidence, she thought bitterly, just as it was no coincidence that Ric Perrini was here in Auckland ushering her to his car.

Perrini was Howard Blackstone's right-hand man, second in command at Blackstone Diamonds, a legacy of his short-lived marriage to the boss's daughter. No doubt her father had sent him to fetch her; the question was *why?*

* * * * *

Get swept away down under with the glitz and glamour of the Blackstone empire as Kimberley tries to determine the real reason behind her "reunion" with Ric….

Look for VOWS & A VENGEFUL GROOM
by Bronwyn Jameson,
in stores January 2008.

When Kimberley Blackstone's father is
presumed dead, Kimberley is required to take
over the helm of Blackstone Diamonds. She
has to work closely with her ex, Ric Perrini, to
battle not only the press, but also the fierce
attraction still sizzling between them. Does Ric
feel the same...or is it the power her share of
Blackstone Diamonds will provide him as he
battles for boardroom supremacy.

Look for

VOWS &
A VENGEFUL GROOM

by

BRONWYN
JAMESON

Available January wherever you buy books

is ringing in the New Year with an innovative new miniseries:

Encounters

One blazing book, five sizzling stories!

Don't miss:

ONE WILD WEDDING NIGHT

by
Leslie Kelly

Girls just want to have fun.... And for five bridesmaids, their friend's wedding night is the perfect time for the rest of them to let loose! After all, love is in the air. And so, they soon discover, is great sex...

Available in January wherever Harlequin books are sold.

REQUEST YOUR FREE BOOKS!

2 FREE NOVELS PLUS 2 FREE GIFTS!

Passionate, Powerful, Provocative!

SDES07

Inside ROMANCE

Stay up-to-date on all your romance reading news!

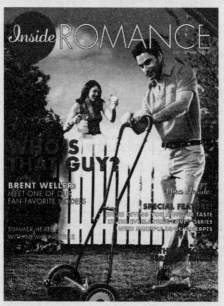

Inside Romance is a FREE quarterly newsletter highlighting our upcoming series releases and promotions.

Visit

www.eHarlequin.com/InsideRomance

to sign up to receive our complimentary newsletter today!

IRN1107

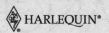

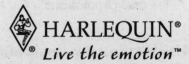

nocturne™

Jachin Black always knew he was an outcast.
Not only was he a vampire, he was a vampire
banished from the Sanguinas society. Jachin, forced
to survive among mortals, is determined to buy
his way back into the clan one day.

Ariel Swanson, debut author of a vampire novel, could
be the ticket he needs to get revenge and take his
rightful place among the Sanguinas again. However,
the unsuspecting mortal woman has no idea of the
dark and sensual path she will be forced to travel.

Look for

RESURRECTION: THE BEGINNING

by

PATRICE MICHELLE

Available January 2008 wherever you buy books.

COMING NEXT MONTH

#1843 VOWS & A VENGEFUL GROOM—
Bronwyn Jameson
Diamonds Down Under
When a scandal overwhelms the opening of his latest diamond boutique, this millionaire proposes that his ex-lover be by his side—not only in the boardroom and the bedroom...but as his wife!

#1844 THE TEXAN'S CONTESTED CLAIM—
Peggy Moreland
A Piece of Texas
He was Texas's wealthiest and most eligible bachelor—and he was also about to uncover the past she'd kept hidden.

#1845 THE GREEK TYCOON'S SECRET HEIR—
Katherine Garbera
Sons of Privilege
To fulfill his father's dying wish, the Greek tycoon must marry the woman who betrayed him years ago. But his soon-to-be-wife has a secret that could rock more than his passion for her.

#1846 WHAT THE MILLIONAIRE WANTS...
—Metsy Hingle
This corporate raider thinks he's targeted his next big acquisition, until he meets the feisty beauty out to save her family's hotel. But what the millionaire wants...

#1847 BLACK SHEEP BILLIONAIRE—Jennifer Lewis
The billionaire's found the perfect way to exact his revenge on the woman who turned him away years ago. Let the seduction begin!

#1848 THE CORPORATE RAIDER'S REVENGE—
Charlene Sands
Seduce his business rival's daughter and gain information on his latest takeover. It was the perfect plan...until the raider discovers his lover is pregnant.

SDCNM1207